Grandpa held up the book so the kids could see the cover. A scary-looking man in a three-cornered hat, with long black hair, a long, curly black beard tied up with ribbons, red-rimmed eyes, a knife in his teeth, and a parrot on his shoulder stared back at them. The kids were mesmerized. "You want me to read this book instead?" Grandpa asked.

"This is Blackbeard," said Grandpa. "He was the bloodthirstiest pirate to sail the seven seas. He was so scary that all the other pirates were afraid of him. Nobody knew for sure what his real name was. Blackbeard wasn't telling. And there wasn't anyone brave enough to ask him. . . ."

The kids leaned forward to listen. They didn't want to miss a thing . . .

The Rugrats Files

A Time Travel Adventure Series

THE Rugrats™ FiLES
A TiME TRAVEL ADVENTURE

YO HO HO AND A BOTTLE OF MiLK

KLASKY
CSUPO INC.

Based on the TV series *Rugrats*® created by Arlene Klasky, Gabor Csupo,
and Paul Germain as seen on Nickelodeon®

ISBN 0-439-23251-1

12 11 10 9 8 7 6 5 4 3 2 1   0 1 2 3 4 5/0

Printed in the U.S.A.   40

First Scholastic printing, November 2000

THE Rugrats™ FiLES
A TiME TRAVEL ADVENTURE

YO HO HO AND A BOTTLE OF MiLK

by Kitty Richards

SCHOLASTIC INC.

New York Toronto London Auckland Sydney
Mexico City New Delhi Hong Kong

CHAPTER 1

"Tommy, what're you doing?" Chuckie asked worriedly as his best friend, Tommy Pickles, rummaged through the refrigerator. Tommy had built a huge pile of books, and he stood on his tiptoes, high on top of a teetering tower. It made Chuckie very nervous. Chuckie was a nervous tyke to begin with. Anything out of the ordinary sent him into a tailspin. And while constructing a stepladder out of encyclopedias and cookbooks certainly wasn't out of the ordinary for Tommy, it was something Chuckie would never think to do—not in a million years.

Tommy poked his head out of the fridge, clutching a head of lettuce to his chest. Dil laughed and pointed at his big brother from his high chair across the kitchen. "I'm looking for eggs, Chuckie," said Tommy. "I just heared Betty say that it's so hot outside, you could fry an egg on the sidewalk! Won't that be so great?"

Betty was Phil and Lil's mom. She was also best friends with Tommy's mom, Didi.

"Ida know, Tommy," said Chuckie. "Your mom might get mad. . . ."

Just then the kitchen door flew open, and Didi and Betty staggered inside. Their faces were red. They looked very hot. Startled, Tommy turned around and dropped the carton of extra-large Grade A organic eggs. *Splat!* Chuckie watched as the eggs scrambled all over the floor. Looking at the yolky mess made him feel a little sick to his stomach. Yuck!

"Look, Deed," Betty said. "It's so hot that the little rascals are trying to get inside the fridge!"

Didi picked up a copy of the latest pamphlet by her favorite pediatrician, Dr. Lipschitz, *Potty Training for Ze Nincompoop*, and fanned herself.

Even with the air-conditioning on full blast, she was still hot.

Phil and Lil trooped into the kitchen. They had been playing Talent Show in the living room with Angelica against their will, and they decided to make a break for it. Being Celebrity Judges wasn't really their idea of fun. They would much rather be outside digging in the dirt and looking for their favorite thing in the world—worms! But as soon as they discovered there were no worms or anything creepy-crawly at all involved in judging a talent show, they quickly lost interest.

Angelica followed close behind them. "Come back, you guys," she called. "We didn't finish playing my game! I was going to sing 'Twinkle Twinkle Little Star' *and* do a tap dance blindfolded. . . ."

Didi did a head count. "One . . . two . . . three . . . four . . . um, where's Susie?" she asked.

Angelica made a face. "She's in the living room doing one of those stupid connect-the-dots puzzles. She thinks she's so great 'cause she knows how to count to twenty-teen!" she said. Angelica suddenly remembered what the adults had been doing outside. "Did you fill the wading pool, Aunt Didi? Did you?" she asked, hopping up and down.

Didi sighed. "I'm sorry, Angelica. I forgot that your uncle Stu poked holes in it for his Giant Colander invention. We couldn't fill it up!"

"What's a collie-der?" Chuckie whispered to Tommy.

"I think it's a big dog," Tommy whispered back.

Angelica started to pout. "But it's so hot outside!" she whined.

Grandpa woke up from his midafternoon nap. He yawned and stretched his way into the kitchen. "You call this hot?" he said. "This is nothing! In my day it was once such a scorcher that the hens laid hard-boiled eggs. And I had to walk *fifteen* miles up a hill to collect 'em!"

Didi sighed as she went to close the refrigerator door, pausing for a moment to enjoy the frosty coolness. "It's brutal out there, Pop," she said. "And you know what the problem is? It's not the heat; it's the humidity. But we have an idea. Betty and I are going down to Pool Palace to pick up a nice new big wading pool for the kids. You wouldn't mind watching the kids inside in the air-conditioning, would you?"

"Nope," said Grandpa. "I've actually got this great book I could read to them. They're never too young to learn all about—"

"You could read them this new picture book from Dr. Lipschitz's Book Club," Didi interrupted. Didi was a huge fan of anything Dr. Lipschitz recommended. "It's called *I'm Okay, You're Even Better*. It's all about fostering self-esteem in children."

Angelica rolled her eyes. She wasn't quite sure what self-esteem was, but it sure sounded boring!

Didi picked up Tommy's little brother, Dil, from his high chair and headed out the door with Betty, her car keys jangling. "See you soon, kids!" Didi called with a wave. "We'll be swimming in no time!"

"And stay out of the fridge in the meantime! We don't want any footprints in the butter!" said Betty with a laugh.

"Whatever you say," answered Grandpa Lou as he settled into his La-Z-Boy and held up Dr. Lipschitz's book. A red-cheeked boy beamed at him from the cover. Grandpa sighed and opened the book. "Let's see," he began. "Okay . . . Little Timmy was feeling blue. 'I'm not as good at baseball as the other kids in Miss Wilson's class,' he said to his mother with a sigh. 'I feel like a failure.' His mom furrowed her brow. 'Why, Timmy,' she said, 'we all can't be good at everything! Why, there are many things that you are quite talented at . . .'"

Grandpa looked up from the book. Tommy was playing with his belly button. Phil and Lil were fighting over their pet worm. Susie was busy doing a new connect-the-dots puzzle. Angelica was humming "Twinkle Twinkle Little Star" and practicing her dance number with her doll Cynthia.

"This is hogwash!" Grandpa said. "Now in my day, kids read real books that kept their attention! None of this namby-pamby feel-good stuff. We liked adventures, and plenty of 'em! And we'd walk *fifteen* miles up a hill to the library to get 'em!" he exclaimed.

Grandpa Lou put down the book and looked at the kids. "I know your mom means well, sport," he said to Tommy. "But the book I have in mind is much better! It's all about adventure on the high seas, swashbuckling pirates, kidnappings, and ransoms. . . ." He pulled out a book from behind the cushion of his recliner. "It's called *The Adventures of Blackbeard, the Bloodthirstiest Pirate to Sail the Seven Seas*," he said.

Grandpa held up the book so the kids could see the cover. A scary-looking man in a three-cornered hat, with long black hair, a long, curly black beard tied up with ribbons, red-rimmed eyes, a knife in his teeth, and a parrot on his shoulder stared back at them. The kids were mesmerized. "You want me to read this book instead?" Grandpa asked.

"Yeah!" Angelica and Susie shouted. Tommy clapped his hands. Phil and Lil gave each other a high five. Everyone was excited to learn all about pirates.

Everyone but Chuckie. He looked like he

needed some convincing. He pulled Tommy off to the side. "You know, Tommy," Chuckie began, "I was really wondering what was going to happen to Little Timmy. He was feeling so bad about himself and all. . . ."

"But Chuckie," said Tommy, "*I'm Okay, You're Uneven Butter* didn't have any bloodthirsty pirates in it!"

"I know," whispered Chuckie. "That's kinda the point."

"Get over it, Finster," said Angelica, interrupting their little powwow. "You're always such a big baby!" She walked over to her grandfather and tugged on his sleeve. "Go for it, Grandpa!"

Tommy and Chuckie toddled back over to the group. Chuckie decided to close his eyes so he couldn't see the mean-looking pirate anymore. "I am not always such a big baby, Miss Angelica Smarty-pants!" he muttered. "I'll show you! When I grow up, I'm going to be a hero!" He thought for a minute. "A *super*hero!"

"This is Blackbeard," said Grandpa. "He was the bloodthirstiest pirate to sail the seven seas.

He was so scary that all the other pirates were afraid of him. Nobody knew for sure what his real name was. Blackbeard wasn't telling. And there wasn't anyone brave enough to ask him. . . ."

The kids leaned forward to listen. They didn't want to miss a thing!

CHAPTER 2

Grandpa began reading:

"Fifteen men on a dead man's chest," sang Captain Kidd.

"Yo ho ho and a bottle of rum!" finished his first mate, Sandy.

"I hate that song," muttered Bucky, the second mate. "Why can't we ever sing nice songs? They're always about dead people and rum!"

Bill and Will, the two deckhands nobody could tell apart, laughed.

The five pirates were in a leaky rowboat, sneaking up on a nearby sailing ship. It belonged to Captain John, who sailed under the flag of his country's king and queen. Lots of times pirates would just sail right up to a ship they wanted to attack and use a large iron hook—called a grappling hook—to pull the ship close. They would then hook, or attach, the ship to the ropes on their sails.

But Captain Kidd and his pirates wanted to be extra careful and use the element of surprise. They had gotten a tip from an informant that this particular ship was loaded with jewels and gold from India—a regular pirate's bounty! This was exactly the kind of treasure the pirates had been searching for for years.

"We're going to be rich!" cackled Sandy.

"The richest pirates around!" said Captain Kidd.

"Yo ho ho and a bottle of rum!" the two pirates sang together.

Bucky sighed.

Captain Kidd had gotten into piracy in a kind of roundabout way. Originally he had been hired to catch the Red Sea Pirates by Governor Bellmont of New York. He then ended up becoming one himself! And a pretty good one, at that—he already had a couple of treasures under his belt. There were even rumors that he had buried a treasure near Long Island, New York, to collect later, but if he had, he was keeping that a secret.

BOOM!

The pirates all looked at each other. Was someone firing a cannon at them?

BOOM! There it was again! It was a cannon, all right, but it wasn't directed at their boat.

"Someone else must be attacking the ship!" cried Will. "Someone will get the jewels and coins that belong to us! We'd better go stop them!"

The pirates rowed faster. There was nothing like a little healthy competition to give them that burst of energy they needed!

When the pirates reached the big ship, they saw another ship anchored alongside it. The flag looked exactly like the one from the big ship. But that was an old pirate trick. Every ship flew a flag. A pirate ship flew a flag called a Jolly Roger. A pirate flag was usually black and white, sometimes with a little red thrown in, the color of blood, and it usually had skeletons, skulls, or crossbones on it. But when a pirate ship wanted to fool a ship into thinking they weren't pirates, they would fly a regular flag to confuse people. It was the oldest trick in the book, but it worked almost every time! It certainly seemed to work this time. . . .

The pirates tied up their boat and climbed up the side of the big ship. When they reached the top, they peeked over the side of the ship. What they saw took their breath away.

"Well, blow me down!" whispered Captain Kidd. It was Blackbeard—the bloodthirstiest pirate to sail the seven seas! Even scary pirates were afraid of Blackbeard. He always carried several daggers and swords and was a scary sight to see! All the ship's passengers, ladies and gentlemen returning from a trip to India, looked terrified. They stood clustered in a group, trembling with fear. No one even dared to raise their eyes to meet Blackbeard's. It was as if they thought he wouldn't notice them, or wouldn't single them out if he couldn't see their eyes!

Blackbeard stood at the front of the boat, waving his sword in the air. He was a huge, loud man. He had the longest, blackest beard that anyone had ever seen. It was tied up with colored ribbons.

"Where is the treasure?" he thundered. "No one will get hurt if you tell me where the jewels are hidden!"

"He's going to get away with our fortune!" whispered Sandy.

"Actually, it's not really ours . . . ," said Bucky.

Grandpa looked up from his book. The kids all sat in a circle, looking up at him with their mouths open. Only Angelica didn't look totally excited. "It's interesting, Grandpa," she said with a dainty little yawn. "But I don't like those scabby old pirates. Aren't there any fairies or princesses in your story? That would make it much more funner for Cynthia and me."

Grandpa smiled. "Patience, my dear," he said. "Just you wait!"

Grandpa continued to read. He told the kids about how Blackbeard told everyone onboard the big ship that they would be sorry if someone didn't tell him where the fortune was! Still, none of the frightened passengers said a word.

"All right!" Blackbeard thundered. "We'll start with you!" He grabbed a small man by the collar. "If no one tells me where that treasure is . . . what's your name?"

"R-R-Randolph P-P-Peterson," stammered the man.

Blackbeard hoisted Randolph Peterson up into the air by his collar. Mr. Peterson's legs dangled in the air. "If no one tells me where the treasure is, Randolph here . . . walks the plank!"

Everyone gasped.

"Unhand that man immediately!" said a voice.

Blackbeard was so shocked, he dropped Mr. Randolph Peterson right on the deck.

"Ouch!" said Mr. Peterson.

Blackbeard was angry! "Who dares to tell Blackbeard what to do?"

"It is I!" said the voice. "Angelique!"

The crowd parted, and a lovely young woman, her golden-haired head held high, faced the fearsome pirate. She looked him squarely in the eye as if to say, You may be bloodthirsty, but I'm not afraid of you!

Blackbeard was shocked. No one had ever spoken to him in such a way before! But he quickly regained his composure. Blackbeard was no fool! Her simple dress did not trick him. He knew who was standing in front of him. It was Princess Angelique. She was not only the fairest, kindest princess in all the land, she was also the sweetest and the bravest. Angelique was known far and wide for her charitable works. She always put other people first.

Blackbeard got an evil gleam in his eye. Forget about finding the jewels—he'd kidnap Princess Angelique instead! The ransom the king and queen would offer for their beloved daughter's safe return would be more than *four* shiploads of treasure!

Blackbeard let out a piercing whistle. In front of the captain's unbelieving eyes, a rope swung over from the other boat. Blackbeard caught it in one hand, tossed the princess over his shoulder, and swung over to his waiting boat.

The five pirates looked at each other.

"Are you thinking what I'm thinking?" said Captain Kidd.

"That we should go home right now?" said Bucky.

"No," said Sandy. "He means that instead of stealing the booty, we should rescue the princess from Blackbeard and get the ransom from the king and queen ourselves!"

"Oh, no," said Bucky. "That doesn't sound like a very good idea at all!" He shuddered just thinking about Blackbeard. If he never saw that bloodthirsty pirate again, that would be too soon!

"Great minds think alike!" said Captain Kidd. "We'll be richer than ever! And the king and queen will be in our debt forever!"

So with that, Captain Kidd and his pirates boarded the big ship and demanded that the ship's captain sail them directly to Madagascar and their ship, the *Adventure*. There they would get supplies and the rest of their crew so they could find Blackbeard and the princess and collect the reward that would rightfully be theirs.

Grandpa read on and explained many things. The kids learned that Madagascar was a beautiful tropical island separated from East Africa by the Mozambique Channel. It was a favorite pirate hangout—because there were always lots of ships on their way to India and China to rob. And there were lots of taverns, parrots, and lots of other pirates—everything a swashbuckler could ask for!

Chuckie leaned over and whispered in Tommy's ear. "What's a washbunker?" he asked.

Tommy thought for a moment. "It's a place where you take tubbies," he said wisely.

When Captain Kidd and his pirates arrived in Madagascar, they couldn't find any pirates who were willing to help. None of the pirates they met on Madagascar were brave enough to help them track down Blackbeard and rescue the princess. Even after they were told of the fabulous riches the king would be sure to give them when his daughter was returned to him safe and sound, they still refused. Blackbeard had an awful reputation. Pirates are mean folks to begin with, but Blackbeard was the meanest. Probably a lot of the stories were just that— made-up stories, but people believed them just the same. It was no wonder no one would join Captain Kidd and his crew!

"Is there anyone who is brave enough to help us?" Captain Kidd asked.

A young boy approached them. "Begging your pardon, sir," he said. "But if you want to meet two of the bravest pirates to ever set sail, you should go to the last ship at the end of the wharf and ask for Anne and Mary."

"Anne and Mary!" scoffed Bill the deckhand. "There's no such thing as women pirates!"

"Says who?" asked a female voice. The pirates all spun around. But wait—were their ears deceiving them? The two people who stood in front of them looked just like pirates— but they sounded like women! All of a sudden Captain Kidd squinted. My goodness! It was Anne Bonny and Mary Read—two of the bravest pirates ever. Because women were not allowed on pirate ships, they had to disguise themselves and dress like men. Legend has it that "Calico Jack" Rackham, their captain, once hid in his cabin while Anne and Mary fought in his place.

Mary and Anne listened to Captain Kidd's tale. They decided they would help the pirates under one condition: The five pirates would first have to help them find a buried treasure. They had found a mysterious treasure map, and they needed all the help they could get to decipher it. Captain Kidd and his crew agreed.

They had not been sailing for long when they spotted a passing ship.

"Ship ho!" shouted Mary.

"And then they suddenly realized . . .," read Grandpa. He yawned. "They suddenly realized . . ." He yawned again. "They suddenly realized that . . ."

CHAPTER 3

"Realized what? Realized what?" yelled Angelica.

There was no answer.

"Grandpa Lou," said Susie hopefully. "What happened next? Do they save the princess? Do they ever get any treasure?"

"Does anyone ever get seasick?" asked Chuckie.

Zzzzzzzzzzzzzzz, snored Grandpa.

"Oh, no!" the kids cried.

"Now we'll never know what happens!" Chuckie said sadly. Phil crawled up to Grandpa's chair and poked him in the stomach.

But Grandpa was fast asleep, the book open on his chest.

Angelica picked up the book and furrowed her brow, pretending to read.

She cleared her throat. "It says here that the princess pushed Blackbeard overboat, and then she took all the jewels and the gold, and all the people on the boat became her boiled subjects, and then they 'lected her president and queen of the world. The end."

Lil looked disappointed. "That story stinks!"

Susie took the book from Angelica and closed it. "No silly, she's just making it up. That's not what happens!"

Angelica scowled. Who did that Susie Carmichael think she was, anyway?

"We want more pirates!" chanted Phil and Lil together.

Susie pretended to be a swashbuckler and started fighting with an imaginary pirate. "Take that, Blackbeard!" she said.

"I know!" said Tommy. "We can be pirates and figure out the ending for ourselves! C'mon, let's go up to my mom's room. She has all sorts of stuff like pirates wear!" Tommy toddled over to the stairs, then turned around and caught Chuckie's troubled look. "Don't worry," Tommy said. "She won't mind!"

The kids trooped upstairs, and Tommy started pulling earrings, scarves, vests, blouses, and all sorts of pirate-ish gear out of his mom's drawers and closets. He found a great pair of shoes with buckles on them. Lil grabbed them, put them on right over her shoes, and clonked around the room.

Phil grabbed an eyebrow pencil from the top of Didi's dresser and drew a curly mustache on his face.

"Me next!" begged Chuckie, forgetting his apprehension for a moment. Phil gave him a handsome beard. Chuckie looked at himself admiringly in the mirror. Then he cringed. Actually he looked a little frightening—he was starting to scare himself!

Susie found that a shoulder pad and a shoelace made a great (if slightly large) eye patch. She walked up to the mirror to see herself, bumping into the furniture. It was hard to see! "What about you, Angelica?" Susie asked, tying a red scarf on her head and attaching a clip-on hoop earring to her right earlobe. "Do you want to wear the other earring?"

Angelica sighed. It was fine for Susie and the rest of the babies to play this silly game—but she and Cynthia were just not interested! "No thanks, Susie," she said. "Thank Bob that I have Cynthia's fashion trunk with me today." She opened it and pulled out a tiny tiara and a dress studded with rhinestones. She dressed Cynthia, and then she reached into her backpack for her own costume.

"What ya got there?" asked Tommy. "Is that your Holly-ween costume?"

Angelica rolled her eyes. Only a baby would mix up a costume with real live princess gear! "No," she said with a sigh. "I never leave home without the tiara I got when I was crowned the Kiddie Queen of Toys Cost-a-lot at the mall!" she said. "That was the happiest day of my life!" She placed the golden tiara on her head and narrowed her eyes. "I am Princess Angelica!" she said. "The brave and beautiful princess who will sacrifice herself for the good of others!"

Susie snorted.

Chuckie laughed.

Angelica ignored them, swirling an imaginary cape around her shoulders. But wait—something was missing. "You don't *all* want to play pirates, do you?" she asked, turning to Lil. In a supersweet voice, she then asked, "Don't you want to be my lady-in-waiting, Lil? It's much better than bein' a scabby old pirate!"

"Nope!" said Lil. "I like bein' scabby!"

"But I have gummy worms!" Angelica said, reaching into her backpack.

"Why didn't you say that in the first place!" asked Lil, grabbing a green one and taking a big gummy bite. "So what does a lady-in-dating have to do?" she asked.

"Oh, the usual," said Angelica. "Obey my every command, eat my vegetables, take naps for me, that sort of thing."

Lil scowled. Well, that didn't sound like fun at all! She handed Angelica back the half-eaten gummy worm. "Well, I quit!" she said. "I changed my mind! I'm going back to bein' a scabby old pirate. They may not give ya candy, but it's more fun!" She turned to Tommy. "I don't have to eat any vegetables to be a pirate, do I?" she asked.

"Nope," said Tommy.

"Yup, I'm a pirate!" said Lil.

Tommy looked at himself in the full-length mirror. The red bandanna around his neck and the blue hat with the yellow feather were just perfect! "All's I need is a parrot," he said. "Then we can sail the eleven seas when our moms get back!"

Once they were all dressed, Tommy opened the treasure chest full of priceless jewels and let everyone take a look at the booty. "Are you sure your mom doesn't mind us playing in her jewelry box?" asked Chuckie.

Just then they heard Didi's car pull into the driveway. They looked out the window. Didi and Betty were struggling to take a huge plastic wading pool off the top of the car.

Grandpa woke up from his nap. "Come on, you landlubbers!" he called from downstairs.

"Time to set sail on the seven seas!"

The kids raced downstairs and went outside to see the new pool. Didi took the garden hose, turned on the faucet—and nothing happened.

Betty turned around and noticed the kids. She let out a loud chuckle. "If I'm not mistaken, one of the pups appears to be wearing your new white silk blouse, Deed," she said.

But Didi was distracted. The hose was all tangled, and she couldn't get the water to come out. "That's nice, Betty," she said. "Silk is such a lovely, all-natural fiber." Finally she straightened out the hose, and the pool slowly began to fill.

Betty reached into a Pool Palace shopping bag and pulled out two big toy ships. "Well, isn't this a great coincidence!" she said, looking at all the kids dressed up in Didi's stuff. "You can't be pirates without these! You should be able to put these to good use," she added.

Lil grabbed the red ship, and Phil grabbed the blue ship as soon as Betty turned her back.

"I want that ship, Philip," said Lil.

"You already have one, Lillian!" said Phil.

"I want both, Philip!" she replied.

Didi picked up another bag. "And wait till you see what I bought!" she said excitedly. "Here's"—she began reaching inside—"the big surprise!"

Phil and Lil immediately dropped their ships. All the kids stared. The big surprise? What could it be?

Didi struggled to open the plastic bag, then resorted to using her teeth. "It's age-appropriate pool fun!" she said, pulling out a huge, squished-looking green thing. "You see, you push this button, and it instantly inflates into the king of all pool toys!" She pushed the button . . . and nothing happened. "But it worked so well at the store," she said sadly. "They said it was so simple, even a child could do it!"

"There, there, Deed," said Betty. "I'm sure you got a defective model. I'll just take it right back there and give them a piece of my mind!"

"Oh well," Didi said absentmindedly, handing it to Chuckie. "Can you hold on to this for me for a minute?"

Chuckie staggered under the weight of the

age-appropriate pool toy, but held on tight. He took all assignments, especially those from grown-ups, quite seriously.

The kitchen door opened, and Grandpa came outside, squinting in the harsh sunlight. He was wearing an old-fashioned–looking bathing suit. It was made of wool and was black with white stripes. It was big and baggy.

"Pop!" said Didi. "That's quite a bathing costume you have there."

Grandpa smiled. "Why, thank you, Didi. And I still fit into it after all these years!" he said. He climbed into the pool. The water barely covered his ankles. "Well, it ain't the old swimming hole we had when we were kids, but it'll do. Very refreshing! You see, in my day—"

"Pop," interrupted Didi. "You won't mind keeping an eye on the kids while we go upstairs to get bathing suits and swim diapers for everyone?"

"Not at all," said Grandpa. He splashed some water on himself to cool off and climbed back out of the pool. He settled beneath a tall oak tree.

Didi and Betty went into the house.

"I'm not wearin' a swim diapie!" said Angelica in a huff. As if!

"Me either!" Susie quickly added.

"I don't want to wear a bathey suit," complained Lil. "I want to skinny flip."

"What's that?" asked Chuckie.

"It's when you take off all your clothings and swim nakie," said Phil.

Tommy picked up one of the plastic ships. "I am Captain Kid," he announced. "Avast there, wateys. Thar she knows!"

"Walk the bangplank!" said Lil to Phil.

"Slob the deck," said Phil to Lil.

"Quiver me timbers," said Susie to Tommy.

Grandpa yawned and stretched out beneath the tree. His eyelids lowered, and he began to doze off.

Chuckie still held on tightly to the squished green thing. "My eye, Captain," he said to Angelica, giving her an awkward salute with his free hand.

"How many times do I have to tell you!" Angelica screeched, stamping her foot. She was really starting to lose patience with everyone. Her Kiddie Queen of Toys Cost-a-lot crown slipped down over her eye. "I'm not a pirate! I'm a princess!"

CHAPTER 4

BOOM!

"What was that?" asked Chuckie. He looked around wildly. He was no longer in Tommy's backyard watching the wading pool fill. He couldn't believe his eyes—he, Tommy, Susie, Lil, and Phil were in a leaky rowboat in the middle of the ocean! They were dressed in their pirate clothes, and Chuckie was still holding on to the squished green pool toy. Tommy and Susie struggled to row the boat. The oars were a lot bigger than they were, which made the job a little tough.

BOOM!

"You guys," said Chuckie. "What's going on?"

Tommy looked around. "Wow! This is neat!" he said.

"Eleven-teen men on a bed man's guest," sang Phil loudly.

"Yo ho ho and a bottle of milk!" finished Tommy.

BOOM! There was that noise again.

"How can you sing at a time like this?" Chuckie wanted to know. "And what is making that scary booming noise?"

Tommy thought for a moment. "It must be Blackbeard firin' a cannon to scare the people on the ship into giving up their treasure, just like in Grandpa's story!" he said.

"Oh," said Chuckie, nodding. Then all of a sudden Tommy's words sank in. "What did you just say?"

"It must be Blackbeard!" repeated Tommy.

"I was afraid that's what you said!" Chuckie said with a gulp.

Despite Chuckie's pleas to go anywhere but toward the boat with Blackbeard on it, the kids rowed the boat over to the big ship. This time it was Tommy, Chuckie, Phil, Lil, and Susie who climbed up the side of the ship, not Captain Kidd, Bucky, Bill, Will, and Sandy. And when they peeked over the ledge, they saw a pirate with a parrot perched on his shoulder talking to the boat's captain. A group of frightened-looking passengers stood nearby.

"He doesn't look all that much like the guy in Grandpa's book," whispered Tommy. This guy was kind of short and a little fat. The parrot that perched on his shoulder was very noisy, squawking away, and it was hard to hear what the pirate was saying. However, Chuckie took one look and almost lost his grip. "He's scarier than I thought!" he said, tightly closing his eyes.

"Is that Blackbeard?" asked Phil in a very loud voice. The parrot stopped squawking, and everyone turned around.

"Uh-oh!" whispered Phil. All the kids ducked so the pirate wouldn't see them.

"Who said that?" the pirate thundered.

"Who said that? Who said that?" echoed the parrot.

"Be quiet, Polly!" said the pirate. "Who said that?" he asked again. Then he smiled a huge smile. "Do you know who I am? It's true: You're looking at Blackbeard—in person!" he announced. "Tell your families and your friends. You've actually met the bloodthirstiest pirate that ever sailed the seven seas!" He seemed quite proud of himself. "Anyone want an autograph? Then I'll commence with the robbing and pillaging, if that's okay."

"I'll take one!" said a voice.

Everyone turned around to see who could *possibly* want a souvenir at a time like this. "Outta my way, lady!" said the same voice. And then Angelica elbowed her way to the front of the crowd. The pirate beamed. He whipped out a quill pen and an 8 x 10 portrait of himself. "And who should I make this out to?" he asked.

The captain of the ship reached over and clamped his hand over Angelica's mouth, but she somehow managed to struggle free. "Make it out to the sweetest, bravest, kindest girl in the land, Princess Angelica," she said, giving the captain a dirty look.

Blackbeard laughed a hearty laugh. "Well, shiver me timbers, if a lovely little princess like you isn't going to bring me a fine ransom of gold doubloons and pieces of eight!" he said.

Angelica beamed. She wasn't sure what gold macaroons and pieces of skates were, exactly, but it was about time someone noticed that she was indeed royalty.

A man, scribbling on a pad of paper with a quill pen, elbowed to the front of the crowd. "Hello there, Mr. Blackbeard, sir, I am Rex Pester, from *Ye Merry Olde Times*. Tell me—the gossip page editor will kill me if I don't ask—do you really have fourteen wives? How do you remember all those anniversaries?"

Blackbeard shook his fist in Rex's face. "Always you blasted reporters! Can't you leave a pirate alone to rob and pillage in peace?"

Rex gulped, but still managed to squeak out, "Can I quote you on that?"

Angelica was enjoying her moment in the spotlight. That's why she was quite surprised when she was unceremoniously scooped up and thrown over the pirate's shoulder. This was no way to treat a princess! "Hey!" she said. "Put me down!"

Just then the cabin door flew open. The ship's cabin boy—a small ten-year-old—stood there, shaking angrily. "Where is that scurvy scoundrel Blackbeard?" he yelled.

"Be quiet!" hissed the captain.

"Let me at him!" shouted the boy. He rushed in the direction of the pirate, but the first mate held him back. The boy stared daggers at the pirate. Then he looked puzzled. "He is way shorter than I thought!" he muttered to himself.

Blackbeard looked at the boy struggling in the first mate's arms. "Hold him back!" he said. "Ooh! I'm scared! Please protect me from that angry little cabin boy!" he said.

Chuckie, Tommy, Phil, Lil, and Susie watched as Blackbeard signaled to his ship. The next thing they knew, his first mate threw Blackbeard a rope, and the bloodthirsty pirate caught it in one hand. "Tell the king that if he wants his daughter back, I want"—he thought for a moment—"six—no, *seven* treasure chests full of gold doubloons and pieces of eight left on Big Turtle Island. I will then make the switch, his daughter for the gold! Otherwise, there's no telling what I will do!"

"No telling what I will do!" the parrot squawked back.

Blackbeard climbed to the side of the ship, jumped up, and swung over to his ship, with Angelica still over his shoulder.

When he landed, Blackbeard gently set Angelica down on the deck of his boat, the *Queen Anne's Revenge*. It was a big ship, one of the biggest pirate ships around. It weighed more than two hundred tons, and was one hundred feet long and had three masts.

Angelica promptly kicked the pirate in the shins! The ships were close enough so that the kids could hear Blackbeard yell, "Owwwwww!" The fierce pirate bit his lip and hobbled away.

"What am I going to do?" wailed the ship's captain.

Rex Pester rushed over to his side. "So tell me, Captain Jonathan, how does it feel to have lost the only daughter of King Drewfus and

Queen Charlotta to the bloodthirstiest pirate to ever sail the seven seas? As I understand it, you report directly to Queen Charlotta herself. Tell me, do you fear for your life?"

The Captain moaned. "I'm finished! The king and queen will have my head, once they find out I've lost their daughter!" He buried his head in his hands.

Rex Pester scribbled away.

"Come on," said Tommy. "We have work to do!" The rest of the kids climbed over the ship's railing and followed Tommy onboard the ship.

Tommy stepped forward and tugged on the captain's waistcoat. "Excuse me, Captain, sir," he said.

The Captain turned around and jumped. "Ahhh!" he said. "A baby pirate!"

"I am"—Tommy thought for a moment—"I am Captain Kid."

"Well, of course you are," said the captain with a bemused look on his face. "And who are the rest of your little pirate friends?"

"This is my first mate, Susie, my second mate, Chuckie, and my deckhands, Phil and Lil.

They're twins," Tommy said.

The captain looked him up and down. "I've had enough pirates for today," he said. "Please go back to your little pirate ship and leave me alone. I have a headache."

"We are here to help you," said Tommy, the new Captain Kid. "I have an idea," he said. "We will rescue Princess Angelica."

The captain looked at him quizzically. "You kids are going up against Blackbeard?" he said. Then he thought for a moment. If the princess were rescued, maybe he wouldn't get in trouble with King Drewfus and Queen Charlotta! "Oh, I mean that's a great idea! I will take you anywhere you need to go. Except . . ."

"We'd like to follow Blackbeard's ship," said Tommy.

"Except that!" replied the captain.

The angry little cabin boy sidled up to Chuckie. "Psst!" he said. "Tell the captain you want to go to Madagascar!"

"Ummm, okay, how about Mad as a Gas Car?" Chuckie suggested to the captain.

The captain thought for a moment. "Why,

that's an excellent idea!" he said. "It's on the way, and you, um, children, will be in your element!" He hurried off to ready the ship to set sail.

"Hi, I'm Grommet," said the cabin boy. "I work here on this ship. I told you to go to Madagascar because it's full of pirates—and I bet lots of 'em will want to help you get even with Blackbeard for all the treasure he's stolen from them over the years!"

"Well, thanks," said Tommy. "But why were you so mad at Blackbeard afore?"

The cabin boy's face darkened. "I'll explain later," he said. "Right now, first things first. We have to get to Madagascar before the captain changes his mind."

Meanwhile, Rex Pester was taking a spot poll for *Ye Merry Olde Times*. "Captain Kid vs. Blackbeard—A Fair Fight or a Lost Battle?" This was the biggest story of Rex's career!

Grommet shielded his eyes from the sun and watched Blackbeard's pirate ship disappear into the horizon. He turned to Tommy. "Are you worried about your friend, Her Royal

Highness?" he wanted to know.

Tommy looked puzzled for a moment. "Oh, you mean Angelica?" he said. "Actually, I'm more worried about Blackbeard!"

CHAPTER 5

"So Grommet, tell us, what ezzackly is a pirate?" Susie decided the trip to Madagascar would be a great time to have all their questions about pirating answered. The kids and Grommet all sat on deck in the warm afternoon sunlight.

Grommet looked at Susie quizzically. Her head scarf and gold clip-on earring looked suitably authentic.

Susie read his mind. "We may look like real pirates," she said. "But believe me, there's a lot we don't know."

So Grommet began with the basics. He

described the different types of people who robbed at sea. "There's a pirate, who robs everyone. There's a privateer, who robs people for his country in wartime and has to give his country a percentage of his booty. Last, but not least, there's a buccaneer, who robs from the Spanish ships, mostly in the West Indies. Many pirates first start out as privateers," he explained. "But when they realize they'll make a lot more money when they don't have to share it, they turn pirate! It happens a lot!"

Phil had an important question. "What do pirates eat?" he asked.

"Oh, on long voyages they'll eat turtle meat, or hard biscuits made out of flour called 'hardtack,' stuff like that. And since water goes bad pretty quickly, they really do drink a lot of beer and rum. Alcohol is the only thing that stays fresh after all that time at sea!"

"Oh!" said Tommy. Maybe being a pirate wasn't all it was cracked up to be!

"Land ho!" someone shouted. They were approaching Madagascar. The kids rushed over to the side of the ship so they could take a look.

Madagascar was a beautiful tropical island that was also a bustling pirate port. It was a huge island separated from East Africa by the Mozambique Channel. As they docked the ship, Grommet told them that Madagascar was known as a "bolt-hole"—a place where pirates could go for refuge when they needed to escape from someone or something. The kids were eager to disembark because Grommet had told them that the island was home to tons of different animals and birds.

"Hurry up! Hurry up!" called Captain Jonathan, as soon as the boat reached the dock. He wanted to drop off the kids as quickly as possible and make a hasty getaway. He wasn't taking a chance on anyone trying to rob his boat again!

Luckily for the kids, Grommet had managed to convince the captain that Grommet should stay with the kids. That way, Grommet told the captain, he would later be able to return to the ship with news of Princess Angelica. However, the captain couldn't see that Grommet had his fingers crossed behind his back because he was telling a fib. You see, Grommet was hoping he'd never have to return to life as a cabin boy again. He was very happy he had run into these new friends! Grommet grabbed his ditty bag, a small bag sailors used to hold their belongings, and was on his way!

The kids stood on the dock, waving good-bye to the ship.

"Thanks, Grommet," said Susie. "We really need your help."

"Well, I really need your help too," said Grommet.

"You do?" asked Tommy.

"You see, I am trying to find my father." Grommet sighed and told the kids his sad tale. "He was captain of a ship for the East India Company. One year ago he set sail on a ship to India. He promised that this would be his last voyage. His plan was to return with enough money so that he could come back to get me and we would live on a beautiful tropical island together. For a while he would write to me all the time, telling me of his adventures. He wrote the best letters too, full of puzzles and riddles for me to solve." Grommet smiled, remembering his father's jokes. "Here's my favorite," he said. "How much do pirates pay for their earrings?"

"Ida know!" said Tommy.

"Me either!" said Lil.

"A buccaneer!" said Grommet. "You get it? A buck an ear?"

Chuckie had no time for jokes. "So what happened to your dad?" he wanted to know.

Grommet sighed again. There was something kind of strange about his new friends. Everyone else he knew laughed at that joke. He continued his story: "But then one day my father's letters stopped coming. I later found out that his ship was attacked by a band of pirates led by none other than Blackbeard! That was quite odd, since no one expected to run into Blackbeard on the Spice Route. He was better known as a pirate of the Caribbean. But I guess the stories of all the treasures from the Far East lured him here. Anyway, it turns out that one of the men in my father's crew was a traitor! He got word to Blackbeard that my father was transporting a fortune in spices and gold. So Blackbeard planned to attack my father's ship, steal the goods, and give the traitor a share of the booty."

The kids all stared, their eyes round with wonder. "So what happened next?" asked Lil breathlessly.

"Was there a big fight?" asked Chuckie. He shuddered at the thought.

Grommet continued. "Well, you know, people think that pirates like to have battles, but the truth is that they mostly like to scare people into giving them their fortunes without a fight. Blackbeard raised his Jolly Roger, which meant there would be no quarter given! That meant that if anyone resisted their raid, they would not be shown any mercy. Usually the captain of a ship about to be attacked would lower his flag to show that they were not going to fight. But not my father! He is a brave, brave man. He would not give up his fortune so easily. This made Blackbeard very angry! So he kidnapped my father and stole the fortune. And what a fortune it was! He had described it all in one of his letters—a ship full of gold, spices, jewels, and silks from India."

"So he kidnapped your dad like he kidnapped Angelica?" asked Phil.

Grommet sighed. "What he did with my father next, no one knows. But I knew my father needed my help. So I ran away and became a cabin boy so I could go to sea and search for him." Grommet got a faraway look in his eyes. "And I will find him, no matter how long it takes."

The kids were all quite sad, Chuckie in particular. "Maybe we can help you find him!" he said. The rest of the kids nodded.

"People tell me to give up. That I'll never find him! But I've come this far. And somehow, I feel that he is near."

"You should never give up," said Lil wisely. "Once I was digging for a worm and Phil said, 'Give up, Lillian, you're never going to find one,' but I didn't give up!"

Grommet nodded. "So you kept looking and you finally found one?"

"Nope," said Lil. "I never found one, so then I

went inside and ate a peeny butter sandwich."

"Oh!" said Grommet. He looked a little confused. But Chuckie had another story to cheer him up.

"Once I was afraid of everything," he said. "And then my dad told me to be brave, and I never gave up, and now I'm only afraid of some things—like icky spiders, and the dark . . . and pirates like Blackbeard."

Grommet smiled. "Thank you, Chuckie," he said. "I'm so lucky that you and your friends came onboard. I've been trying to get to Madagascar for months, but Captain Jonathan was always too scared to come here. He is not a brave man like my father!" He leaned forward and whispered, as if Captain Jonathan were standing nearby, "Just between you and me, I think he's *really* afraid of Queen Charlotta!"

At the dock they watched some pirates loading their ships with supplies. Other pirates were onboard their ships repairing their rigging (the ropes) and the sails. They saw a pirate walk by with a crate full of limes. "What are those for?" asked Tommy. Grommet explained that lots of pirates—and sailors—used to suffer from a disease called scurvy, because of the lack of citrus fruits at sea. So before long voyages, they learned to stock up on limes to get their vitamin C. That's why British sailors are sometimes called limeys.

"Ewwww! Limes is yucky!" said Lil. "I ate one once accidentally. I thought it was a green orange." She made a funny face, just thinking about it.

Grommet took them from ship to ship, introducing them to all sorts of famous pirates. The first thing he did was ask if any of the pirates had heard of his father. A couple of them had heard of Captain Ben Blunderbuss, and that he was a good guy, for a non-pirate. But they only knew the same story Grommet knew: That the ship had been attacked by Blackbeard and that Captain Blunderbuss had never been heard of again. Grommet told some pirates that they were on a quest to find the princess. At first everyone was interested in rescuing Princess Angelique and collecting a reward. But as soon as they heard the name

"Blackbeard," they all suddenly had different plans.

Grommet shrugged and stopped at another ship. "I am quite sure that John Taylor will help us!" he said confidently. "He holds the record for the largest pirate prize ever: a ship with over one million British pounds' worth of cargo!"

The kids boarded the ship and found John Taylor busily polishing his telescope.

"Are you a buckaroo?" Phil asked him.

Taylor just stared at Phil.

"We hear you are a brave and strong man!" said Grommet. He thought maybe this time he would try flattery.

"I am!" said John Taylor, holding his telescope to his eye. Apparently it wasn't clean enough. He frowned and continued polishing it.

"We have heard that you have captured more pirate's booty than the rest of all these pirates combined!" Grommet exclaimed, motioning to all of the different pirates coming and going below them on the dock.

Taylor smiled. "I have!" he said.

"And that you fear nothing!" Grommet continued.

"I don't!"' said Taylor.

"Good!" said Susie. "Then you won't mind helping us track down Blackbeard!"

"Blackbeard!" shouted Taylor. He nearly dropped his telescope overboard. "Um, I'm too busy! I have to wash my hair!" he said.

"But you haven't taken a bath in two and a half years!" said his first mate, who was swabbing the deck nearby and overheard his boss's lame excuse.

"Well, wouldn't you say it's about time?" Taylor shouted back at the deckhand.

The kids all shook their heads. Who would have thought all these brave pirates would be such ninnies! And people called *them* babies!

Dejected, the kids decided to drop into one of the taverns to try to find some milk. All of this searching was making them pretty thirsty. "And who knows," said Grommet. "Maybe we can find a pirate to take us on his ship. I doubt we have enough money to charter a ship, but maybe if we promise to share the reward money for Princess Angelica's safe return, we can strike a deal!"

"Sounds like a great idea!" said Susie. And the rest of the kids agreed.

The kids soon realized that Madagascar had its fair share of taverns. Laughter and music drifted out to the street from each one.

"Pirates sure like to sing!" Lil noticed.

"They sure do. Sometimes onboard the ship they sing sea chanteys," said Grommet.

"What's a sea chantey?" Susie asked.

"Sea chanteys are songs that help them keep a rhythm so everyone can do their work around the ship together," explained Grommet.

As the kids passed one tavern, The Admiral Benbow Inn, they heard a somewhat familiar song:

Ninety-nine bottles of punch on the wall,
Ninety-nine bottles of punch!
If one of those bottles should happen to fall,
How many bottles of punch on the wall?

"Life on the sea is hard," explained

Grommet. "It's a lot of work, sometimes there are bad storms, and it also can get very boring. So when the pirates arrive at tropical ports with the money they got from robbing other ships, they can sometimes spend it all in one night eating and drinking in the taverns! They stay up all night singing and playing cards and having fun and then the next day they have to go out to sea again and make more money!"

There were so many places to choose from—The Salty Dog, The Regal Beagle, The Yardarm, The Dewdrop Inn, The Jolliest Roger. Finally the kids all decided to go to The Yo-Ho-Hole in the Wall.

The kids all walked into the tavern. Pirates were playing cards, talking, and laughing. As soon as they saw the kids, silence fell over the room.

"Who's that kid?" an old man with an eye patch wanted to know. He was pointing straight at Tommy.

"Hello, I'm Captain Kid!" said Tommy. "Ahoy to you all!"

The kids bellied up to the bar. "What's your

poison?" asked the tavern keeper.

"Oh, no poison, thank you," said Chuckie. He stared at the man. Why in the world would they want poison? "We'll all have milk."

The tavern keeper shrugged and filled six leather cups with milk. "Tavern keepers use these leather cups because pirates can't break them!" explained Grommet.

Tommy picked up his cup. "These look like sippy cups!" he said.

Once the kids had gotten their milk, they all sat down at a table. A gruff-looking pirate with a wooden leg sat down across from Tommy. He held a deck of cards, which he shuffled in one hand. It was a neat trick. "What's your game?" asked the pirate.

Tommy told him.

"Never heard of it," said the man. "But I'm a fast learner." He dealt the cards, and they started playing.

"You got any of these cards with the king man on them?" Tommy asked.

"Go fish!" said the pirate.

Tommy won the game easily, and soon all

the pirates wanted him to teach them this new game. Tommy also showed them how to play Old Maid. And then, before the tavern keeper knew it, he was out of milk because everyone wanted some!

Phil and Lil taught everyone how to blow bubbles in their milk and make milk mustaches. And Susie taught everyone the words to "Old MacDonald Had a Farm." All the pirates thought it was the best sea chantey they had heard all year. A pirate played "The Sailor's Hornpipe," and Phil and Lil started to dance. Pretty soon everyone joined in.

When everyone sat down to rest, Susie seized the moment. She climbed up on a table and got everyone to quiet down. "Attention!" she said. "We are looking for a few good pirates to join us on an adventure!"

"Sign me up!" called one pirate.

"Me too!" said another. "You guys are so much fun!"

"So where are we going?" asked a man whose arms were covered in tattoos.

"We're going to rescue a little princess who

has been kidnapped!" Susie announced.

"Awwwwwwww!" said everyone.

"And we might get a huge reward!" she said.

"Ooooooh!" said the crowd. A reward sounded good!

"What lily-livered coward kidnapped this princess?" one of the pirates asked.

"Susie," whispered Grommet. "I'm not sure you should—"

"Blackbeard!" announced Susie.

A hush fell over the crowd. And suddenly, everyone rushed out the door!

The place was empty in no time!

The kids all stared at each other in disbelief.

"Where did everybody go?" said Tommy.

"Was it something I said?" Susie asked.

CHAPTER 6

"It happens every time," said the tavern keeper as he wiped off the bar top. "Someone mentions the name 'Blackbeard' and it clears the place out!"

"Is Blackbeard really as awful as they say?" asked Susie.

"Well, I'll just tell you this," said the tavern keeper. "He came into my friend's tavern once and ordered the Seaman's Special—all the dried turtle and hardtack you can eat—and then he left without paying! He's a scoundrel, all right!"

"You know," said Susie, "that Blackbeard

doesn't sound like anything else 'cept a big bully!"

"Bullies is mean!" said Chuckie with a shudder.

Tommy nodded. "Susie is right," he said. "Blackbeard is just a big bully. Like that kid at the playground who wouldn't let you go in the sandbox, 'member, Chuckie?"

Chuckie nodded solemnly.

"And then 'member, we all got together, me and Susie, and Phil and Lil, and even Angelica, and we told him to stop bein' a big old mean bully, 'member what happened?"

Chuckie grinned. "He started to cry!"

"So bullies aren't really so bad," Phil said.

"They're really just big babies," said Lil.

The kids all nodded wisely.

"I have an idea," said Grommet. "We haven't spoken to *every* pirate on Madagascar yet. I heard two pirates talking last night about this secluded cove where pirates take their ships to clean them. I got directions from them. It's kind of a dangerous job, so maybe we'll find a brave pirate there."

They started walking along the beach.

"By cleaning, you mean they sweep and polish their boats?" Susie wanted to know.

"No, I mean they clean the outside!" said Grommet. "When a ship is in the water, lots of seaweed and barnacles get stuck to the bottom of it. This slows down the boat a lot, and then the ship can't escape quickly when it needs to. Also, there are these worms, called teredo worms, that love to eat the wooden hulls of boats for lunch. So after the pirates remove the barnacles and seaweed, they cover the bottom of the boat with sticky stuff to keep the worms out."

They turned onto a path that led into the rain forest. "You see, a regular boat, like the one I was on, can be dry-docked for cleaning—you know, it is completely pulled out of the water. But pirates don't have the tools we have. They have to beach their boats to clean them. So they do it in very secluded areas, like this cove I'm taking you to."

What a remarkable place Madagascar was! As they walked through the forest, they saw plants and birds and animals they had never even heard of before!

"What's that?" asked Phil, pointing to a tree with a wide, odd-looking trunk.

"That's a bottle tree!" said Grommet. "Its trunk is the same shape as a bottle!"

Grommet showed them sweet-smelling vanilla plants, and a plant that ate bugs after it attracted them with its pollen. "Look at all the different kinds of bugs!" said Lil, prying a big rock out of the ground.

Tommy saw a blue chameleon skitter by. "Wow! I didn't know they came in blue!" he said.

"That must be Reptar's little brother!" said Chuckie.

"Here's something really amazing," said Grommet, pointing to a rather ordinary-looking plant. "This plant is called the traveler's palm. If you are ever lost in the rain forest, you can always get a drink of water from it at the bottom of its leaf stalk. It is filled with fresh water and has saved many a thirsty traveler!"

In a clearing, Lil noticed a huge flock of

bright pink birds. Most of them were standing on one leg. "Flabingos!" she said. "Wow, there's so many of them!" She stood on one leg and tried to balance herself.

All the kids joined in and soon they were all hopping around. "Whee! I'm a flabingo!" cried Chuckie.

"Let's keep moving!" said Grommet.

After a long but interesting walk, they arrived at the cove. There was, indeed, a ship on its side, being scrubbed down by a crew of pirates.

"What's that smell?" asked Tommy, wrinkling his nose.

"It's the stuff I told you about that protects the boat from that worm. They're covering the bottom of the boat with it," said Grommet. "It's a mixture of tar, sulfur, and tallow."

Grommet studied the ship. "I'm pretty sure that is Captain Bart Roberts's boat," he said. "I recognize his Jolly Roger. He's known as Black Bart and he's from Wales. He was forced into piracy, but he soon became a very fierce pirate. They say he has captured four hundred ships!"

"Well, maybe he's ready to capture four hundred and one!" said Susie. "Let's go find out!"

Grommet approached a deckhand who was hard at work scrubbing away at the hull. "If you please," Grommet said, "we'd like to talk to Black Bart."

The deckhand turned around, saw a group of kids standing there, and laughed rudely. "Black Bart don't have time for the likes of you!" he snarled. "He's busy!"

"Well, we were wondering if he would help us track down Blackbeard the pirate," said Grommet.

All of the color left the deckhand's tanned face. "Um, did I say that Black Bart was busy? I meant to say he isn't here!" he said. "He's on vacation! Come back later!" The deckhand backed off and ran away.

The kids walked away from the beached ship to a deserted stretch of sand and sat down dejectedly. The soft, white sand, the warm tropical breeze, and the turquoise blue waters were all so pleasant and beautiful, but they hardly noticed. Grommet shook his head. He picked up some pebbles and angrily tossed them into the surf. "No one has any information about my father, and no one will help us find the princess. What are we going to do?"

Lil sighed. She decided she would cheer herself up by doing her favorite thing—digging. If there wasn't any mud, sand would have to do. "I'm going to bury you, Philip!" she said.

"Not if I bury you first, Lillian!" Phil said, starting to dig his own hole. He paused for a moment. "That John Taylor guy may have been wimpy, but he was pretty neat! One good thing about bein' a pirate," he said. "No baths!"

"Get ready to be buried by Lillian, girl pirate!" said Lil.

"Hey!" said a voice. "Look—little girl pirates!"

"Kind of brings a tear to my eye," said another voice. "Just look at what we've started!"

Everyone spun around to see who was talking. And there stood two people dressed head to toe in pirate gear. The kids looked closer—they looked like all the other pirates they had seen, with one difference. These pirates were women!

"My goodness!" Grommet exclaimed. "Well, if it isn't Anne Bonny and Mary Read!" He jumped up and shook their hands enthusiastically. "It's an honor to meet you!" He frowned. "But last I heard, your ship was captured by the British navy, and you and the entire crew, including your captain, Calico Jack Rackham, were thrown in jail!"

Anne laughed. "Do you really think there's a jail big enough to hold the two of us?" she asked.

"I guess not!" said Grommet with a laugh.

Grommet turned to the kids to explain the famous story. "When the officers came onboard, all the other pirates onboard, including Calico Jack, were cowards and hid. But Mary and Anne fought valiantly."

"That we did!" said Anne. "And we would have escaped too, had our crew fought alongside us. Unfortunately we were outnumbered and were captured. But we managed to escape soon enough, and here we are!"

"But I thought that you mostly sailed around the Caribbean," said Grommet.

"We usually do," said Anne. "But we are on the trail of a treasure chest! In the Caribbean we befriended an old pirate who had found a mysterious treasure map in this area. But he hadn't been able to decipher it. Since he wouldn't be returning to the Indian Ocean, he gave us the map. So here we are loading up for what we hope will be our final pirate adventure. If we find this treasure chest full of treasure, we can retire."

"Retire?" said Grommet. "Don't you like being pirates?"

Anne sighed. "After that close call, we decided to change our lives and give up looting and pillaging and stealing from others."

"But you're our last hope," said Susie. "The bloodthirstiest pirate to sail the seven seas stole our friend Angelica because he thinks she's a princess. But really she's just the Kiddie Queen of Toys Cost-a-lot," she explained.

The women looked puzzled. "The Kiddie Queen of what?" asked Mary.

"So you needs to help us!" said Tommy. "We gots to get her away from Blackbeard! Before one of them gets hurt!"

"Blackbeard!" said Mary Read. "Why didn't you say so? He owes us money! The last time we were in Saint Kitts, he said he forgot his wallet on his ship, and we had to spring for his tavern bill! He told us he'd send us the money, but he never did! Of course we'll help you!"

"It's a deal!" said Tommy.

"So meet us at our ship in half an hour," said Anne. "We're going to pick up the newest member of our crew. Luckily, since we cannot make heads or tails of this map, we met a man last night named William Wexford, who claims to be the best treasure map decipherer in Madagascar. He has helped many a pirate find buried treasure."

"I almost forgot," said Tommy. "There's one more thing. Our friend Grommet here losted his daddy. So we gots to help him too!"

"It's a deal!" said Anne and Mary together.

"Great!" said Tommy. They were finally heading off on a high seas adventure!

CHAPTER 7

"Welcome aboard, swabbies," one of the deckhands said as Captain Kid and his crew boarded Mary and Anne's ship.

"Thank you, and you look very scurvy today!" said Lil, trying out some pirate talk herself.

The deckhand looked a little upset.

"Lil," whispered Grommet, "you should never tell a pirate he looks like he has scurvy!"

"Oh," said Lil. "I mean you look very good today!" she said.

The kids could see Mary and Anne talking in the corner with a thin young man with a big mustache.

"This is William Wexford, our map expert," they said, walking over to greet the newest members of their crew. "He's going to help us decipher the map and find the treasure."

"Pleased to meetcha," said Tommy.

William eyed Grommet. "Have we met before?" he said. "You look very familiar to me."

Grommet shook his head.

"What's your name?" William asked.

"Grommet," said Grommet. "Grommet Blunderbuss."

The map specialist seemed to turn pale. "You know," he said to Mary, "a pirate ship is no place for children. They will just get in the way. We should leave them behind."

"Not going to happen," said Mary. "These kids are staying."

"Noisy kids!" muttered William as he went below deck to start deciphering the map.

After they set sail, Mary asked Tommy if he wanted to try steering.

"Sure!" said Tommy. He stood at the helm, steering the boat under Mary's watchful eye.

While Tommy sailed, Grommet gave

Chuckie a tour of the boat, explaining all the different parts to him. He told him that the front of the boat was called the bow; the back of the boat was called the stern. The right side of the boat was the starboard side (not the "starfish" side), and the left side was the port side (not the "sport" side). "Tommy is standing at the bridge, steering the boat," continued Grommet, "and we are all standing on the deck. The hold is where the cargo is carried, and the hull is the main part of the ship."

Tommy was having a great time steering the ship. Mary grinned at him. "You're doing a wonderful job, Captain Kid," she said. "You're a better sailor than a lot of grown-up pirates I know!"

Grommet was done with his ship lesson and was standing at the bow of the ship, scanning the horizon. Suddenly he saw something. "Look!" he cried. "I have heard tales of these half-fish–half-woman creatures, but this is the first one I've ever seen."

Phil, Lil, and Susie leaned forward to see. In the distance they could barely make out a figure. They squinted. It looked kind of like a woman bobbing in the waves, cradling a baby.

"Lookie!" Lil cried. "It's a mermaid! Maybe we could take her home and puts her in our bathtub, Philip. Mom said it's time we gets a pet!"

Mary laughed and laughed. She walked over and handed Grommet a telescope. "You kids have fallen prey to one of the oldest sea legends there is!"

"Are you certain?" said Grommet. "I could swear it was a woman. . . ." But then he looked through the telescope and got a better look. "Oh, I guess you're right," he said sheepishly. "It looks like some kind of animal!"

"It's a manatee," said Mary. "A lot of people think they are mermaids. I think from a distance they mistake a mother manatee holding her baby for a woman cradling a child. How a sea creature with whiskers becomes a beautiful fish-woman with long hair is a mystery to me. But believe this, there's no such thing as a mermaid!" She saw Grommet's disbelieving look. "And while we're on the subject, there's no such thing as a sea monster, either," she explained.

Grommet did not look convinced. He eyed her warily. "But all the deckhands on Captain Jonathan's boat told me stories all about the horrible monsters of the deep! Surely there are sea monsters!" he protested.

Mary laughed. "Most of the so-called sea monsters that people have spotted are actually giant squid."

"Really?" said Grommet. "How big are they?"

"They can grow up to fifty feet long!" said Mary.

"My goodness!" said Grommet. "I would certainly be afraid to come face-to-face with a giant squid! That would seem enough like a monster to me!"

Mary and Anne were very generous captains. They allowed all the kids to have a turn sailing the ship. Phil and Lil argued over who was the better sailor.

"I am definitely better, Lillian," said Phil.

"Are not!" cried Lil.

When it was Chuckie's turn, he saw something

funny surface near the boat. It was some sort of an animal with a long, spiral tusk. The tusk appeared to be made of ivory and was almost eight feet long. It was the oddest thing Chuckie had ever seen in his life. "It's a municorn!" he shouted.

Anne laughed. "Actually, that's a narwhal!" she explained. "It's a kind of whale. I can tell it's a boy narwhal—can you guess why?"

"No. How do you know?" asked Chuckie.

"Because only male narwhals have tusks," said Anne. "It's really just a very big tooth!"

"Wow!" said Chuckie. "I bet he's got a really big teethbrush!"

"I'm going to check on our map expert," said Anne. "If he's such an expert, surely he must be close to finding the secret of the map by now. Do you want to come with me, Chuckie?"

Chuckie nodded.

When they got downstairs to the galley, Anne and Chuckie found William sitting at a table surrounded by code books, instruments, and tons of reference books. He stared at the series of numbers on the page that were set up in an odd formation, almost like a shape. "What can these numbers mean?" he muttered. "Is it latitude? Longitude? Miles? They must be special coordinates I need to figure out. . . ." He looked about ready to throw the map out the porthole into the sea.

"Dare I ask how it's going?" said Anne.

William glowered at her.

"Do you need any help?" she asked gently.

"That's it! I've had enough! This map must be a trick! There is no treasure! This is impossible!" William was yelling and throwing books about the galley. Up above on the deck, everyone could hear him yelling, "This is the toughest map I have ever seen! I give up!" He stomped off to his cabin.

Anne and Chuckie walked back on deck. Anne was holding the map. "He's not close, he's not close at all," she said. She shrugged. "He's supposed to be the best. Maybe this map is impossible to decipher?"

Mary sighed. "We might as well anchor now, Anne," she said. "There's no use sailing any farther if we don't know what direction we're supposed to go in."

Anne shrugged. "Okay. Hey! We're right near Pleasant Cove. Why don't we go for a swim?"

"Yippee!" shouted the kids. That was a great suggestion. It was a hot day, and the clear turquoise waters looked so inviting. Mary sailed to the cove.

"That reminds me of a joke my father used to tell," said Grommet. "When is a pirate ship not a pirate ship?"

Silence.

"When it turns into a cove!" he said.

Once again nobody laughed.

After they set anchor, everyone went swimming. Everyone except William, who was snoring away in his bunk. He was exhausted!

The kids all climbed down the rope ladder that hung from the side of the boat, and jumped off the last rung. The water was turquoise blue and as warm as a bathtub.

"Whee!" said Lil, splashing everyone.

Phil and Lil picked up handfuls of delicate shells. Tommy and Chuckie chased the colorful fish that swam around their legs.

"I love bein' a pirate!" Susie shouted as she jumped off the rope ladder for the tenth time. "This is amazing!"

"This is amazingly terrible!" said Blackbeard. He watched as his entire crew sat cross-legged on the deck of the boat, having a pretend tea party with Angelica. It was almost too much for the bloodthirsty pirate to bear!

"Would you like sugar in your tea, ma'am?" Angelica asked the big, bearded second mate.

"Yes, please, Princess Angelica," he said, holding out his imaginary cup for a lump. Blackbeard stared in disbelief. His brave, burly second mate actually held his pinkie out gracefully as he took a pretend sip of tea!

Blackbeard paced the deck. "How long do we have to wait before we go to Big Turtle Island to collect those gold macaroons, I mean gold doubloons?" he muttered. Blackbeard sighed. He had been through some tough times, battled some of the fiercest pirates in the world, done more than his fair share of kidnapping. And yet this little princess was too much for him!

He turned to Angelica. "I am Blackbeard—the bloodthirstiest pirate to ever sail the seven seas!" he thundered.

"Ooh, stop it, you're scaring me!" said Angelica with a giggle. Blackbeard wasn't sure, but he thought he might have heard a couple members of his crew giggle too. He sighed loudly. All that time spent terrifying his crew into submission—down the drain!

Blackbeard had had enough! "I'm going to take a nap!" he shouted. "Wake me up when this is all over! I have a headache!"

"I have a headache! I have a headache!" repeated Polly. Blackbeard smiled at his beloved parrot. At least *she* was loyal!

"Take a nap," said Angelica.

"Take a nap!" Polly squawked. "Take a nap!"

Blackbeard stared in disbelief as his pet immediately flew off his shoulder and landed on Angelica's shoulder.

"You too, Polly?" he said with a sigh.

CHAPTER 8

After their afternoon swim, everyone had dried off and was lounging on deck, waiting for William, the treasure map expert, to wake up and get back to work. The kids were surprised to see that many of the deckhands were playing games.

"Aren't they too growed up for games?" Lil wanted to know.

"Oh, no," said Grommet. "Lots of pirates play games to make the time go by faster. I told you life at sea can get pretty boring."

The first mate was carving a nautical scene into a shell with a knife. Tommy watched in amazement as he worked tiny details onto the small canvas. "It's called scrimshaw," said the first mate. "Lots of times sailors carve on bones, teeth, or tusks—whatever materials they find on shore."

Chuckie wasn't looking at the scrimshaw. He was too busy admiring the first mate's golden earring. "Is it a clip-on like Tommy's?" he wanted to know.

"Nope," said the man. "It's real!"

Grommet told him that lots of sailors believed that wearing gold in your ears improved your eyesight.

Pretty soon Tommy and Chuckie were in the middle of a game of tiddledywinks. Lil and Grommet joined in on the game. The second mate sat in the sun practicing various nautical knots—the figure eight, the clove hitch, the square knot—and Phil watched him carefully. "Lil had better watch out now!" said Phil with a grin.

Susie decided she wanted to draw and grabbed a bunch of paper she found on deck. She fished a crayon out of her pocket and started drawing some pictures. She decided that since she didn't have a camera with her, she would draw everything she had seen so far. Then a page with a drawing already on it caught her eye. "All right!" she said, and immediately went to work.

Anne put down the book she was reading, *How to Succeed in Pirating without Really Trying*, and wandered over to see what Susie had drawn.

"Oh, look! A narwhal!" Anne exclaimed, studying Susie's drawing. "Very nice!" She picked up another picture. "And look here, we have a manatee. And here's a picture of William having a fit. . . ." She shuffled through the pages, then suddenly stopped. She looked at the paper, blinked hard, looked at it even closer, and gasped. "Well, knock me overboard and send me to Davy Jones's Locker!" she exclaimed.

Mary jumped up, dropping a deck of cards. She had been playing Go Fish with Tommy. "What's wrong?" she asked.

Anne held up the paper. "Look at this!"

87

Mary gasped, then covered her mouth with her hand. "Could it be?" she asked.

Anne nodded wordlessly.

"Well, blow me down!" said Mary, shaking her head and looking at Susie.

Just then William appeared on deck. His hair was sticking up funny from his long nap. "Well, back to work," he said.

Anne stuck the paper in his face. "Look at this!" she said.

"I can't believe it!" he shouted. "One of those darn kids wrote all over the treasure map!" he yelled. "I knew you shouldn't have allowed them onboard!"

Anne shook her head. "No! Don't you get it?" she said. She turned to Susie. "By George, I think *you've* got it!" she said.

"By Georgie, I've gots it!" Susie exclaimed. Then she looked puzzled. "Gots what?"

"You solved the secret of the treasure map!" exclaimed Mary.

"Let me see that again!" William said, grabbing it out of Mary's hand. "There's no way a mere child could have cracked a code that I couldn't figure out. . . ." He squinted at the paper. He turned it right, left, and then upside down. Then his face turned as white as a sheet. He stared at Susie. "You *have* solved it! Are you a genius or something?" he asked.

Susie laughed. "Of course not, silly!" she said. "It was just a big old connect-the-dots puzzle! All you hafta know is your numbers!" She grinned. "I just learned 'em, you know. Angelica doesn't even know her numbers yet!"

"I always thought Susie was a beanius," said Tommy solemnly. He toddled over and looked at the map. When the dots were connected, it formed a picture of a big turtle.

"Who would have thought!" said Anne. "The treasure we've been searching for is on Big Turtle Island!"

"Hooray for Susie!" Everyone cheered. William, no longer the treasure map expert, scowled.

"Moist the sails!" said Tommy. "Starfish to bangplank! Next stop Big Turtle Island!"

Everyone went straight to work, hoisting the sails, weighing the anchor, and charting the coordinates. They were on their way to find buried treasure!

A deckhand sailed the ship while everyone bustled around locating shovels, picks, and all sorts of treasure-finding gear. Lil and Phil found some sacks they thought would be great for filling up with jewels.

Tommy stood on the bow, the wind blowing across his scalp. The sails billowed. What an exciting adventure this was turning out to be! But they had only been sailing a couple of minutes when Grommet suddenly noticed a ship approaching.

Mary grabbed the telescope from Grommet and studied the ship. "Oh, no!" she cried.

"What's wrong?" asked Susie.

"I know that ship—it belongs to a bounty hunter, a privateer. Certain countries and some companies hire them to hunt down and capture pirates. Oh, we're doomed. You know, there's a big bounty if Anne and I are brought in because we escaped from jail. And, of course, we've done our fair share of robbing and pillaging over the years!"

"Let's sail away!" suggested Susie.

"Oh, no, we can't," said Mary. "That boat is a single-masted sloop and would catch up with us in an instant!" she said. "Our boat is a heavier schooner—it can travel in shallower waters than most boats and get away. But if we took off right now, that would make them very suspicious. We have to stay calm and hope for the best."

Anne nodded in agreement. "Our best bet is to not act suspicious, and hope they leave us alone!" She shook her head. "It's pretty nerveracking, though." She looked around at everyone. "Oh, no!" she said. "Take off your pirate gear! Quickly!"

Everyone removed their hats and scarves from their heads and golden earrings from their ears, trying to look as un-piratish as possible.

"All right, we're all set!" said Mary.

But then the first mate remembered their ship's calling card. "Oh, no!" he wailed. "We forgot to take down the Jolly Roger!"

"Well, it's too late now!" said Anne. "The

boat is too close! There's no time!"

Everyone held their breath as they watched the boat approach. Then it just passed them by, the privateer himself giving them a cheery wave as his ship passed by!

Everyone breathed a huge sigh of relief.

"How did that happen?" Mary said, shaking her head in disbelief.

"It's a miracle!" said Anne. "How he saw our Jolly Roger and still kept on going is a mystery to me. . . ." Then she looked up at the flag—and laughed out loud.

"What's so funny?" asked Mary. Then she looked up too, and began to laugh herself. For instead of their unmistakable skull and crossed swords flag, a plain white one flew in its place.

"No, it's not a miracle!" Anne said. "Someone took down the flag and put a new one in its place! But who did it?"

"It wasn't me," said the first mate.

"Me either," said the second mate.

"Then who was it?" said Mary. "I command whoever took down the Jolly Roger to make him or herself be known immediately."

There was a moment of silence, and then Chuckie timidly raised his hand. "It was me," he said softly. "I'm sorry. I didn't mean to take down your flag." Chuckie thought he was in trouble for doing something wrong!

"Chuckie, you saved us!" said Mary. "That was some pretty quick thinking."

All of the other members of the crew shook their heads. "I wish I had thought to do that!" said the first mate.

"Really?" said Chuckie.

"Hip hip hooray!" said the crew, lifting Chuckie up on their shoulders.

"But how did you know what to do?" someone asked.

Chuckie turned red and looked at the floor. "I *didn't*," he said. "My diapie got wet when we was swimming, so I took down the flag and put it up to dry! I thought it was a clothesline!"

"Super," said Anne.

"Our hero!" said Mary.

Chuckie beamed. "I've always wanted to be a superhero," he exclaimed.

CHAPTER 9

Tommy, Chuckie, Phil, Lil, Susie, and Grommet all stood on the ship's bow, scanning the horizon for a glimpse of land. They could hardly contain their excitement. They were hot on the trail of pirate treasure!

"I've heard tales of treasure chests full of diamonds and rubies and emeralds!" said Grommet. "Maybe we'll even find some beautiful rare black pearls from the bottom of the ocean." He smiled, just thinking of what might be in store for them. "And of course gold doubloons and pieces of eight."

"I've been wonderin'," said Tommy. "What

ezzackly are gold balloons and those geeses of eight things?"

Grommet smiled. "Gold doubloons and pieces of eight are Spanish coins," he said. "Gold doubloons are gold coins. Pieces of eight are silver coins. They are also called pesos."

"Wow!" said Tommy. "Gold, silver, *and* sparkling jewels!"

"Maybe," Grommet mused, "if we find this treasure, Anne and Mary will split some of the booty with us. Then I will have enough money to buy my own ship and hire a crew to help me find my father!"

"Anne and Mary seem like very fair pirates to me," said Susie. "I wouldn't be surprised if they did just that."

"I bet the treasure will be worth a bazillion dollars!" said Lil dreamily. "And I will buy a hunnert Reptar Bars with it!"

Phil smiled. "I would buy enough gumdrops to last forever. Or maybe till affinity," he said. "But only red ones—they're my favorite."

"I would give the treasure to my dad," said Chuckie. "But first maybe I would get myself one Dummi Bears video. Or maybe five. And maybe enough Reptar Cereal so I could have it for breakfast every day for a year!"

"Land ho!" called the second mate from high up in the crow's nest. The kids all squinted into the distance, trying to make out the island, but it was hard to see with the naked eye. After a little while they too could see the land before them. They were approaching Big Turtle Island.

"Look out, treasure," said Tommy. "Here we come!"

The first mate anchored the boat. Mary and Anne gathered the shovels and stuff they would need. There was a brief discussion about just how many sacks they would need to transport the treasure back to the ship. They finally decided on four. Chuckie, Phil, Lil, Susie, Tommy, Grommet, Anne, and Mary climbed into the rowboat, and the crew lowered it into the water. William Wexford scowled. He hated being left behind!

When they got close enough to the sparkling white beach, Mary jumped out and pulled the boat onshore. Everyone disembarked. Big Turtle Island was a smallish tropical island with lots of palm trees, beautiful flowers, and chattering birds.

"Look! I see a monkey!" warned Chuckie, watching one swing through the trees. After their adventure in a forest a while ago with a pack of banana-hungry monkeys, he was kind of nervous. But, he noticed with a sigh of relief, there appeared to be a nice supply of bananas on this island.

Anne and Mary studied the map, their brows furrowed. Phil and Lil ran up and down the beach. It felt good to be back on firm ground. Susie discovered some funny, sideways-walking crabs and played hide-and-seek with them, chasing them back into their holes. Chuckie liked standing in the shallow water watching tiny minnows swim around his toes. Tommy and Grommet stood close by the two pirates in case they needed any help.

Mary gave a whistle, and everyone gathered around her. She opened the map, and everyone leaned in close for a look. "Well, this is the beach we are on, right here, next to the turtle's head, and there's a big arrow next to a group of three palm trees. Do you think the treasure is right here on this beach?" Mary asked.

Everyone looked up. There were three palm trees, clustered together, on the far side of the beach.

"Well, let's go see," said Grommet.

Everyone started looking all around the palm trees. Phil spotted an envelope on the back of the middle tree! "Lookie here!" he cried. "I think it's a clue!"

Mary reached up and grabbed the envelope. "Good job, Phil!" She tore it open and unfolded the clue. She furrowed her brow. "It's just a riddle," she said. "A kid's riddle."

"Read it, Mary!" said Susie.

"Okay," Mary said. She cleared her throat. "What happens when you throw a blue rock into the Red Sea?"

Susie knew her colors as well as she knew her numbers. "Does it turn purple?" she guessed.

Grommet laughed. "I know! When you throw a blue rock into the Red Sea, it gets wet!"

"But what does that mean?" asked Anne.

Grommet thought for a minute. "I think it means we're supposed to find a blue rock on this beach."

Everyone groaned. The beach was covered with rocks!

They all started searching. They found gray rocks, and black rocks, and white rocks. Some rocks looked reddish, and some looked pink. They looked for a long time. Finally, they sat down on the sand to take a rest. Tommy put his hand down—right on a blue rock!

"I gots a blue rock!" Tommy shouted. It was a big one, and he could hardly pick it up. Mary rushed over to help him. She turned it over. It was painted blue, and there were some words printed on it.

"What does it say?" asked Susie. She may have mastered her colors and her numbers, but not reading—not yet, anyway.

Mary read the rest of the directions. "It says we should walk fifty paces southwest and look under a bush that is shaped like a seal." She pulled a compass out of her pocket and flipped it open with her thumb.

"Look—it's a crumpus!" said Lil.

When Mary had figured out what direction they were supposed to be heading in, everyone started counting and pacing. Some were better at counting than others.

"One . . . two . . . three . . . four . . . five . . . six . . . seven . . . eight . . . six . . . twelve-teen . . .," Tommy called out. Everyone stopped, completely confused.

"Hey, wait a minute," said Anne, after a moment. "I have an idea. Why don't I count and the rest of us just follow along?" Everyone thought that was a good idea, and they started over. Soon they were standing in a clearing filled with bushes of all shapes and sizes.

"This one looks like a seal—if it had two heads!" said Phil.

"This one looks like a big moosie," said Tommy.

Lil went from bush to bush, looking at them carefully. Finally she stopped at one. She squinted. Why, it looked almost exactly like a seal, its nose held in the air. She dropped to the ground and started poking around underneath it. Her hand touched something hard and cool. "I finded something!" she yelled out to the others.

Everyone came rushing over. Lil held an old-fashioned–looking key in her hand. Attached to the key was a note. She unfolded it.

"Look—pitchers!" she said. It was a rebus puzzle.

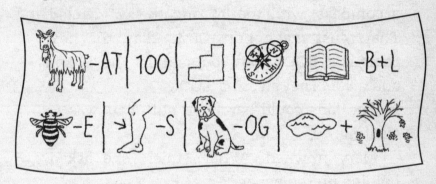

Lil handed Mary the note. "Okay, everyone, put your thinking caps on," she said. She held up the note. "What does this look like?" she asked, pointing to the first picture.

"A goat!" they shouted.

"Okay, so you take 'GOAT' and subtract 'AT,' and you get the word 'GO,'" Mary said.

Anne scribbled that down.

"Okay, the next thing is the number 100. Write that down, Anne."

Anne did.

"Here is a set of stairs. And what are stairs made up of?" she asked.

"Steps!" everyone shouted. Anne scribbled away.

"And here's a picture of a crumpus, I mean, a compass, with the 'N' and the 'W' circled. That must mean northwest. Okay, the next thing is a 'BOOK,' but you subtract the 'B' and add an 'L.' That gives us 'LOOK.'"

The kids could barely sit still. This was so exciting!

Mary frowned. "What's this?" she asked, holding up the paper. "A fly?"

Tommy took a closer look. "Looks more like a bee," he said.

"I think you're right!" she said. "Good one, Tommy! Now here's a leg. There's an arrow pointing to a part of the leg. It's not the knee, it's not the ankle—"

"It's the 'SHIN'!" said Anne. "Minus the 'S,'

that leaves 'HIN.'" She wrote that down too.

Phil stood up to get a better look at the next clue. "That's a doggie!" he shouted.

"That's right, Phil! Minus the 'OG,' that leaves 'D,'" Mary said.

Everyone agreed that the next picture was of "WATER." The last picture was a little confusing. It was of a tree that was losing its leaves.

"Is it winter?" Susie guessed.

"Autumn?" wondered Anne.

"I gots it! I gots it!" said Lil. "It's 'FALL.'"

Everyone studied the notes that Anne had taken. It looked like this:

GOAT 100 STEPS NORTHWEST LBOOK BEESHINDOG WATERFALL.

Anne studied it. "Go 100 steps northwest. Look behind waterfall!" she cried.

Everyone did just that. This time they let Mary do the counting from the beginning.

Soon they were standing in front of a beautiful waterfall. The water cascaded into a pool at the bottom. Mary did a little exploring and discovered there was a walkway behind the waterfall. The walkway was slippery, so they all had to walk very slowly, single file.

"Hey, look! There's a cave!" cried Tommy. Everyone filed in. When their eyes adjusted to the darkness, they could see there was an "X" made out of pebbles on the ground.

Mary and Anne unpacked the shovels. Everyone took turns. They dug for quite a while. Not surprisingly, Phil and Lil were the best diggers of them all. Everyone rested while the two of them dug away. "Whee!" said Lil. "This is so much fun!"

Clang!

"I think we found the treasure chest!" said Lil. Mary and Anne jumped into the hole and finished digging. Together they lifted out a huge, battered chest.

Tommy took a close look at it. "It's locked!" he said. Lil used the key she had found under the bush. The lock was rusty, but it finally clicked open. *Screech!* It worked!

"Wait a minute!" said Mary and Anne.

Everyone paused. "We just want to say that this treasure will be divided evenly among us!" they said. "It's the Pirate Rules of Conduct, you know. I know we're all pirates, except for you, Grommet, but we are also very honorable. You have all helped us find this treasure, and we shall share it equally."

"Yippee!" shouted Lil. "Reptar Bars, here I come!"

"Thank you!" said Grommet.

Tommy slowly lifted the lid of the treasure chest. Everyone leaned forward to see what the treasure was.

Everyone stood there, just staring. Mary whistled. "Wow!" she said.

Inside was a glittering fortune of gold doubloons!

CHAPTER 10

"We're rich! We're rich!" shouted Phil and Lil.

Everyone started jumping up and down, whooping and yelling.

Mary picked up Tommy and gave him a hug. "Thanks to you and your friends, now we can retire! No more pirating! No more hardtack! I never liked that stuff very much—no flavor!"

"No more robbing and looting!" said Anne. "This is the happiest day of my life!"

"Me too!" exclaimed Grommet. "Now I will be able to find my father!" He picked up two handfuls of gold coins and threw them into the air. They fell all around him like gold raindrops.

"And we can use our share for Angelica's ransom!" said Susie. "This is great!"

"These monies is yummy!" said Lil. Everyone stopped dancing and looked over at Phil and Lil. Gold and silver foil littered the ground. Their faces were smeared with chocolate.

"Oh, no!" cried Mary. "It can't be!"

"Yes, it is," said Phil. "And it's *delicious*!"

Everyone stood there in shock. Their glittering treasure-filled chest was merely a box of foil-covered chocolate!

Grommet looked very sad. "I need to be alone right now," he said. Everyone watched as he walked out of the cave, his shoulders sagging with disappointment.

"Poor Grommet," said Tommy. "He wanted the monies to be real 'cause he needs it to find his dad."

Everyone sighed. They all felt bad that the treasure wasn't real, but they weren't nearly as upset as Grommet.

Susie peeled the gold wrapping from a "doubloon" and popped it into her mouth, then took another look at the so-called treasure chest. She noticed something she hadn't seen before. "Hey, look," she said. "It says something on the inside of the chest."

"What does it say?" asked Mary.

"Um, don't know. I can't read," said Susie with a shrug.

Anne and Mary bent over and leaned forward to read the message.

"How odd," said Mary.

Everyone gathered around.

"What's it say?" asked Tommy.

"It says, 'Gotcha,'" answered Anne. "What could that mean?"

The next thing they knew, a big net fell over their heads from above. They were trapped!

"It means exactly what it says," said a big, loud voice. "Gotcha!"

"One . . . two . . . three . . . four . . . five. . .," counted the first mate on Blackbeard's ship. He leaned against the ship's wheel, his arm covering his eyes as he counted away.

"But, Princess Angelica!" Blackbeard whined. "I don't want to play hide-and-seek!"

"Hide!" commanded Angelica.

"But I don't want to!" he said.

"Hide now!" Princess Angelica narrowed her eyes. Why was Blackbeard such a party pooper? He was always raining on her parade! She'd found the best hidey place ever for him. "Hide up there!" she said, pointing to the crow's nest, high above the deck.

"Up there?" whispered Blackbeard.

"Uh-huh," said Angelica firmly.

"But, I'm"—Blackbeard ran a finger under his tight ruffly collar. He looked around to make sure none of his crew was listening— "afraid of heights!" he hissed.

Angelica stared at the bloodthirsty pirate. "Hide now!" she said.

A deckhand, who was crouched uncomfortably in a nearby apple barrel, poked his head out and said, "You'd better do it, Captain. Remember the ransom!"

Blackbeard took a deep breath and began climbing the high ladder to the crow's nest.

"We're leaving for Big Turtle Island as soon as this stupid game is over!" he said. "I can't take this anymore!"

"Shhhhhh!" commanded Princess Angelica. "Climb!"

"Climb, climb, climb," screeched Polly from her favorite perch on Angelica's shoulder.

Blackbeard sighed, took a deep breath, and began climbing.

"What happened?" asked Phil. "Who caught us?"

"I don't know!" Mary said, trying to pull the net from over their heads.

"Well, the old fake-treasure-map-in-a-bottle-trick finally worked!" said the voice. It was a man's voice.

"So the whole thing was a trick to lure us to this island so you could capture us?" asked Anne.

"Well, yes it was," said the man. "And pretty clever too, don't you think?"

"Clever, yes," Mary agreed. "But very disappointing! May we remove this net now?"

"Certainly!" said the man. "Just no false moves. Since I finally got you here, I want to make sure you don't leave without me!"

Mary and Anne pulled the net off of everyone. They could finally catch a glimpse of the person who had captured them. A man with long hair and a bedraggled beard stood before them, grinning from ear to ear. He had obviously been on the island for a long time. He was quite tan, he wasn't wearing any shoes, and his clothes were almost in tatters.

The man sat down on a nearby rock. "You have no idea how happy I am to see other human beings! The monkeys here are all quite nice but, no offense to them, it's just not the same, you know." He shook his head. "I was marooned here months and months ago by a dastardly pirate who left me here without even a single book, can you imagine? So I spent my time coming up with puzzles and riddles to keep myself busy. What do you think of this new riddle I just came up with: What is the only thing you can put into a bucket that will make it lighter?"

Everyone guessed.

"Feathers?" tried Mary.

The man shook his head.

"Water?" asked Tommy.

"Nope."

"Ummm, bug juice?" asked Lil. Everyone gave her a funny look. What was bug juice? It didn't sound very good!

"I know! I know!" said a voice. "The only thing you can put into a bucket that will make it lighter is a hole!" Everyone turned around to find Grommet standing at the mouth of the cave. The light behind Grommet was dim, and it made it hard to see him.

"That's right!" said the man with a big smile.

It took a minute for Grommet's eyes to adjust to the darkness of the cave. When his eyes could focus, he suddenly gasped. He tried to speak, but couldn't.

"What's wrong?" Anne asked worriedly.

Finally Grommet's voice started working again. "Can it be?" he shouted. "Father, is that you?"

"Heavens above! Do my eyes deceive me?

Could that be my little Grommet?" the man cried. "My goodness, you have grown!"

"It's Grommet's missing daddy!" shouted Lil. "Thank Bob!"

Grommet and his father hugged each other very hard.

"I never gave up!" said Grommet. "I kept looking and looking! I knew you were out there, I just knew it!"

"Wow," said Tommy. "It's a family re-onion!"

Grommet introduced everyone to his long-lost dad, Captain Ben Blunderbuss. Then Captain Blunderbuss took everyone to the little hut he had called home for the past eleven months. "Built it myself!" he said proudly. There was only one chair, so everyone sat on the ground. "I wasn't expecting company!" Captain Blunderbuss said with a smile. "I hoped for some, of course, but I thought that constructing extra furniture seemed a little optimistic!"

Everyone laughed, even the kids, who had no idea what "optimistic" meant.

After everyone had made themselves comfortable, Captain Blunderbuss told his story.

"I was on my way back home from my final voyage to India. I had finally sailed enough trips for the East India Company and, with this last haul, I was going to have enough money to retire. The plan was that I was going to sail home to pick up Grommet, and then we were going to live on a tropical island together. I couldn't wait to go home and see my son. And then we were attacked by pirates! None other than Blackbeard himself. I knew then that one of my crew had been a traitor and had told Blackbeard exactly where he could find us and all about the goods we had onboard. Well, I wasn't giving up the fortune without a fight. Unfortunately, our ship was overpowered. Blackbeard decided to punish me. He thought it would be a funny joke to maroon me on this island with nothing but the treasure chest full of chocolate coins I was bringing home as a souvenir for Grommet. Lucky for me it turned out to be a tropical paradise! I wouldn't have minded spending the rest of my days here, but I missed my son." He paused and smiled at Grommet, ruffling his hair.

"So when did you decide to make a fake treasure map?" asked Susie.

"Well, luckily I had a bunch of bottles with me. Every week I would write messages begging whoever found it to come rescue me. But no one ever did. Finally, I was down to my last bottle. I realized that the only way to be rescued was to create a treasure map, directing whoever found it to this island. Then I waited to be rescued. And in the meantime, to keep myself busy and to amuse myself, I created the treasure hunt."

"Well, it did work!' said Anne. "I'll give you that."

Everyone listened to Grommet's father's story, transfixed. What adventures he had been through!

"If only I could see that dastardly villain Blackbeard again!" said Grommet's dad. "He owes me a fortune—and an apology!"

Everyone laughed.

"What's so funny?" Captain Blunderbuss wanted to know.

"Well, you're in luck!" said Tommy.

Back at the ship, everyone was disappointed that the treasure was a fake. But they were really happy that Grommet had found his father. Someone lent Captain Blunderbuss some fresh clothes, and he borrowed a razor and a pair of scissors. He was in his cabin for quite a while. When he stepped back on deck, hardly anyone recognized him!

"Now there's the father I remember!" said Grommet happily.

William kept staring at Ben Blunderbuss, but would look away whenever the captain looked back at him. Finally Captain Blunderbuss asked, "Do I know you? You look so very familiar to me."

"Never seen you before in my life!" replied William hastily. He stroked his mustache nervously. "Never seen you before!"

Anne, Mary, and Grommet's dad got together for a conference. When they were done, they called everyone on deck for a ship meeting. Captain Blunderbuss did the talking. "We are about to undertake a dangerous voyage," he began. "We are going to go after the bloodthirstiest pirate that ever sailed the seven seas."

William raised his hand. "I don't think that's a very good idea, actually."

Everyone ignored him.

"Blackbeard is a very sneaky man," Captain Blunderbuss continued. "It will probably take us a long while to track down this scurvy scoundrel, but no matter how far we have to go, we will find him. We will search all four corners of the world, we will leave no stone unturned in our quest, we will devote our lives to hunting down this evil menace and saving this poor, harmless princess. We will search day and night, night and day to put an end to his reign of terror. . . ."

Meanwhile, Grommet had been trying to get his father's attention. He pulled on his sleeve. "But when we find him, and we will . . . yes, Grommet?"

Grommet pointed to the ship that was quickly approaching them. "I think we found him," he said.

Everyone gasped and scrambled to the side

of the ship. Sure enough, the *Queen Anne's Revenge*, Blackbeard's ship, was approaching them. His Jolly Roger with the skeleton holding a sword, a heart, and an hourglass was flapping in the wind. Blackbeard himself steered the vessel.

Captain Blunderbuss blinked. "Um, okay, here he is," he said. He cleared his throat. "There will be no quarter given!" he shouted. "Let the battle begin!"

CHAPTER 11

Everyone waited, holding their breath, as the dreaded pirate's ship approached. A battle with Blackbeard was a scary thought. Would it begin with flaming arrows? Cannonballs fired at them? Or would it be a sneak attack? Tommy, Susie, Phil, and Lil were at the ready. Chuckie was expecting the worst.

"Is everyone all set?" Anne asked. "Hey, where is William? We need all hands on deck!"

Everyone looked around. William was nowhere to be found.

"Coward!" said Grommet. "I bet he's hiding under his bed!"

The pirate's ship got closer . . . and closer . . . and closer.

"Any minute now . . .," said the Captain.

"Ahoy there!" shouted a voice. It was Blackbeard. He stood at the side of his ship, not waving a cutlass or a sword but a white flag—the white flag of surrender!

He waved at everyone with his free hand. "Hi, there!" he called out rather politely. "May I have a word with you?"

Mary and Anne looked at each other. Could they trust this scoundrel? "Okay," they said warily.

"I wanted to talk to you about Princess Angelica's ransom," he said.

Tommy, Susie, Chuckie, Phil, and Lil held their breath. What would Blackbeard ask for? All they had was a treasure chest full of chocolate. Surely that would not be enough to appease a pirate like Blackbeard! What were they going to do?

"Would you like it all in gold doubloons and pieces of eight, or would you like some jewels too?" Blackbeard wanted to know.

Anne and Mary stared at him in disbelief. What was going on? Was this a trick? No one knew how to respond.

Just then Tommy stepped forward. "Ida know," he said. "How much you gots? It's gonna take a lot for us to take her back!"

"Hey!" said Angelica with a scowl, suddenly appearing on deck at Blackbeard's side. Everyone stared. Instead of wearing her princess costume and gold tiara, she was dressed from head to toe in pirate gear!

"Oh hi, Angelica!" said Tommy. "No offense, but it's gonna take a lot of booty for us to take you back!"

"I just don't get it," Phil whispered to Lil.

"Me either," said Lil.

"Does he know what he's doing?" the first mate whispered to Anne.

"Oh, I think he knows *exactly* what he's doing!" said Anne with a grin.

"All right, fine!" shouted Blackbeard. He was starting to get nervous. "I'll give you gold doubloons, pieces of eight, *and* jewels. Just take this princess off my hands *now!*"

Tommy told Blackbeard he'd consider the offer, but that he had to think it over.

Blackbeard squinted in the sun and shielded his eyes with his hand. "Captain Blunderbuss, is that you? How are you doing?"

Captain Blunderbuss cleared his throat. "Well, Blackbeard, I'm a little bit better now that I'm no longer marooned on Big Turtle Island."

Blackbeard slapped the heel of his hand to his forehead. "I was trying to remember the last time I saw you!" he said. "That's right, I marooned you there! Well, that wasn't very nice of me, was it?" He thought for a moment. "I'll throw in an extra sack of gold doubloons for your trouble!"

"What else?" said Tommy. He was playing hardball and enjoying it!

Blackbeard started searching through his pockets. "All right," he said. "I'll even throw in this lovely pocket watch." He held it up for them to see.

"That's *my* watch," Captain Blunderbuss said coldly. "You stole it from me before you marooned me. I never knew what time it was for eleven months!"

Blackbeard was getting desperate. He searched his pockets. "How about my lucky shell?" he said. "Come on, I can't take it anymore! I need to take back control of my crew!"

Tommy softened. "All right, you give us the treasure, two extra sacks of gold doubloons, the watch, and we'll take the princess back!" He thought for a minute. What was that naughty-cal 'spression? "And I'm not givin' ya any quarters!"

"It's a deal!" said Blackbeard. "Send over a rowboat!"

The first mate climbed into the boat and rowed over, and the next thing they knew, Angelica was on her way back. In the boat next to her was the treasure—many sacks spilling over with gold doubloons, silver pieces of eight, and jewels!

Blackbeard explained himself. "I think I realized I had to get rid of the princess when she had a beauty contest and all my crew joined in—happily! Or maybe the last straw was when she replaced all the figure eights and square knots with bows because they looked prettier. All the sails ended up falling down on my head!"

Everyone had to snicker at that one.

"Anyway, it was time for her to go home," he said. He looked at Tommy and shook his head. "Shiver me timbers, Captain Kid, you sure do drive a hard bargain!" Blackbeard paused for a moment. "But it is worth it. I had no idea just what a talented crew I have. Seeing that beauty pageant really opened my eyes. We've all decided to give up pirating. We're on our way back to Madagascar to start Blackbeard's Pirates of the Caribbean Dinner Theater!"

"I never knew I had stage presence until Angelica pointed it out," said the first mate. He waved to the princess. "Good-bye, Princess Angelica. I'll miss you!"

Angelica's boat reached their ship. Mary reached down to help her onboard. The first mate stared unloading the booty. And what a treasure it was!

"Angelica!" said Lil. "Why are you dressed

like a scabby old pirate?

Angelica shrugged. "If you can't beat 'em, join 'em. 'Sides, you can't climb the rigging in a princess dress!"

Blackbeard waved as he took off. "Hey, everyone, you can all have free seats to opening night of my show! Just make sure to check your daggers at the door!"

Everyone laughed and waved.

And as Blackbeard departed, Polly flew over to his shoulder. "Angelica is number one! Angelica is number one!" she squawked.

Angelica grinned.

"Arrrrgh!" groaned Blackbeard. "That's it—I'll never work with kids or animals again!"

After dinner that night, everyone sat around talking about the adventures they had had. A fake treasure. A real one. A rescued princess, a found father. It had been quite a day!

"I'm sleepy," Susie said with a yawn.

"Well, we can all bunk up," said Mary. "Except we need someone to do anchor watch tonight to make sure that the boat does not drift. Any volunteers?"

"I'm not tired!" said Captain Blunderbuss. "I don't mind staying up!"

"Me either!" said Chuckie. "I can keep you company."

Everyone headed downstairs to various bunks and hammocks while Chuckie and Captain Blunderbuss settled onto the deck. After a while Captain Blunderbuss realized he was hungry and went below deck to get a midnight snack. Everyone was sound asleep. Chuckie looked up. The night sky was filled with glittering stars—more than Chuckie had ever seen before in his life. They looked so close, he was tempted to reach up and touch one. Then he saw a shooting star. He gasped. What a beautiful night this was!

Suddenly Chuckie thought he heard something. He listened harder. Was that a splashing sound? What could it be? He peered over the side of the ship. Was it a school of fish? A dolphin dancing in the moonlight? A map expert making off in the dead of night with the treasure? Chuckie couldn't believe his eyes.

In the moonlight he could see William Wexford, treasure map expert, sitting in the rowboat, the glittering pile of coins and jewels next to him.

"Stop!" called Chuckie. "Help!" he cried. "Captain Ben, come help!" But it was no use. No one could hear him above the waves, slapping at the side of the boat.

That wasn't fair! Mary and Anne had promised everyone onboard part of the booty, and this guy was stealing it all! It belonged to everyone, not just him. Chuckie looked around wildly. What could he do to stop him? Suddenly he saw something out of the corner of his eye. Something large and green and squished looking. Without even realizing what he was doing, Chuckie picked it up, staggered over to the side of the boat, hoisted it to the edge, and hurled it as hard as he could. *Splash!* It hit the water and . . .

WHOOSH! The pool toy instantly inflated.

"Ahhhhh!" yelled William. For in front of him was the biggest, meanest dinosaur ever to roam the earth. The squished-looking green thing had inflated into a huge Reptar pool toy!

"Sea monster!" shouted William. "Help me, it's a sea monster and it's going to eat me!"

In a panic he stood up in the boat. Then he lost his balance and tumbled into the sea. "Help me!" he cried, before he went under. "I can't swim!"

CHAPTER 12

Chuckie ran to the steps that led down to the galley and yelled, "Captain Blunderbuss, come quick. Man overboat!"

Captain Blunderbuss ran up the stairs holding a plate of food. He dropped it, and it clattered to the deck. He tore off his boots and dove overboard.

The screaming and yelling woke up the entire ship. Everyone straggled on deck in their pajamas and rushed to the side of the boat to see what was going on.

"Is that map guy being attacked by a sea monster?" asked the second mate.

"I think so!" said someone.

"But sea monsters don't exist!" Anne kept shouting. "They're commonly confused with giant squids!"

"The map guy is being attacked by a giant squid!" shouted the second mate.

"A giant squid! Is my father okay?" asked Grommet worriedly. "Where is he?" He peered anxiously over the side of the ship.

"It's okay!" Captain Blunderbuss's voice rang out. "William is fine. And it wasn't a sea monster!"

Someone lowered the Jacob's ladder, and William Wexford was helped onboard. A blanket was wrapped around him. He was shaking. "A terrible sea monster attacked me!" he said.

"Do you mean this?" said Captain Blunderbuss, climbing over the side of the boat. He placed the giant inflated Reptar pool toy on the deck. Everyone gasped.

"Thanks to Chuckie's quick thinking, this man was not able to steal our treasure!" explained Captain Blunderbuss. The two deckhands raised the rowboat back onboard.

William had been trying to get away with the *entire* fortune!

"You're a thief!" Angelica shouted.

Captain Blunderbuss stepped forward and took a close look at William. His thick mustache was now hanging on only half his lip. It was a fake! The captain ripped it off.

"Ouch!" said William.

"I know you!" the captain shouted. "William Wexford, map expert, my foot—you're Billy Bones, the traitor! I didn't recognize you with that fake mustache. You're the crook who set me up and let Blackbeard rob my ship!" He turned to the rest of the crew. "No wonder he couldn't figure out the treasure map! He was the galley boy on my ship!"

Billy scowled. "Don't think you're the only seaman who wants to retire. Do you have any idea how boring it is to work in the galley, peeling potatoes all day long? After I told Blackbeard about the fortune on your boat and he robbed you, I was supposed to meet him in Madagascar and get my portion of the booty. But that dishonorable pirate never showed up!

So I worked in a tavern on Madagascar, waiting for another treasure to steal. When I overheard Mary and Anne talking about their map, I posed as an expert so I could get onboard their ship. Things weren't going well, but then when Blackbeard gave you that fortune, I couldn't believe my luck!" He paused and looked at the kids. "And I would have gotten away with it if it weren't for you . . . you . . . babies! That red-headed one in particular!"

"Chuckie saved the day—again!" shouted the first mate. "He saved the fortune. Hip hip hooray!"

Once again the crew hoisted Chuckie onto their shoulders.

"You guys!" said Chuckie. "Okay, you can stop throwing me now! Please stop!"

"Chuckie's a hero?" said Angelica in disbelief. "I didn't know the little guy had it in him."

The next day everyone sailed to Madagascar, where they dropped off Billy Bones. They were glad to be rid of him!

"I have an idea!" said Susie. "Why don't we have a party to celebrate?"

"And I can be the guest of honor," said Angelica.

Everyone ignored her.

"That's a great idea!" said Anne. "But where should we have it?"

"How about back on Big Turtle Island?" suggested Captain Ben. "I know I don't have a lot of chairs, but we can have a big clambake on the beach. It'll be great fun!"

"Are you sure you don't mind going back there?" asked Mary. "You were marooned there against your will, after all."

Captain Blunderbuss sighed. "Actually, I kind of miss it," he said. "I'd love to go back one last time, if the rest of you don't mind."

Everyone agreed that Big Turtle Island would be a great place to have a party. They picked up supplies and were on their way.

The party was a great success. Captain Blunderbuss was in charge of the clambake, and there was lots of great food—clams, and lobsters, and potatoes, and corn on the cob. Some of the crew were musicians, so there was music and dancing after dinner. The kids' favorite dance was the limbo, which they did all day long until they were pooped. Everyone was very impressed with how low Chuckie could go!

Finally, everyone sat around on the beach, quite full and tired.

"I love this place," said Anne.

"Me too!" said Mary. "I feel like we belong here."

"I never want to leave!" said Grommet.

"I don't, either!" said Captain Blunderbuss. He jumped up. "I have an idea!" he said. "Why don't we all live here? Instead of dividing up the treasure, we can pool the money and settle here!"

"That's a perfect idea!" said Mary. "Maybe we could even set up a haven for seamen and other pirates who are willing to give up robbing and want to live in peace in a place where they can relax and tell their stories."

"Wonderful!" said Anne. "What do the rest of you think about giving up pirating and settling here?"

"Count me in!" said the first mate. The rest of the crew cheered. Everyone wanted to stay!

"How about you and your crew?" asked Anne.

Phil spoke up. "What time do ya have to go to bed around here?"

"Anytime you want," replied Anne.

Phil and Lil looked at each other, interested.

"And can ya watch cartoons before breakfast?" Lil wanted to know.

Mary frowned. "What are cartoons?" she asked.

The twins shrugged. "Oh, well," said Phil. "Guess we'd better go home, then."

Tommy agreed. "We'd love to stay with you guys," he said. "But I think our job here is done. And we'd probably better get home soon. Our moms and dads will start to worry."

"Okay," said Anne. She looked sad. "We will miss you. But remember that there's always a place for you on Big Turtle Island."

Grommet came over and gave each of them a big hug. "I can't thank you enough for helping me find my father. You've made me the happiest boy in the world!"

"You are a brave bunch. Especially you, Chuckie," said Mary.

"It's true," said Captain Blunderbuss. "I'd still be alone on this island if it weren't for all of you."

The kids walked over to the punch bowl. "Now the question is, how do we get home?" asked Susie.

"Ida know," said Tommy. "It's a mystery to me!"

"Anyone want some punch?" asked Chuckie, pouring himself a cup. The fruit punch suddenly started to spill out of the bowl, all over his shoes.

"Watch out, Chuckie! You're spillin' the punch!" said Susie.

Chuckie had a strange look on his face. He backed up. "It's not me, you guys!"

The kids stared. Sure enough, the punch was bubbling out of the punch bowl, overflowing and spilling onto the floor all by itself!

CHAPTER 13

"What's going on?" said Chuckie. Suddenly he looked around. He was no longer on the shore of Big Turtle Island, his feet getting splashed by passion fruit punch. He was in Tommy's backyard, but his feet were still getting wet. He looked down. It was the swimming pool that was overflowing!

Grandpa, who had been under the tree daydreaming about the swimming hole of his youth, snapped to attention. "Oops!" he said. "I guess I let it fill a little too much!" He stood up, walked over, and turned off the faucet. Didi and Betty arrived just then with swim diapers and bathing suits for everyone.

"Who's ready to swim?" Didi said cheerily. She placed the two ships in the water. "You can sail the seven seas with these lovely sloops!"

Susie gave the ships a closer look. "Actually, they're schooners," she said.

Just then Didi noticed Reptar, which sat on the ground near the pool. "Look, Betty!" said Didi. "Chuckie inflated the Reptar pool toy all by himself." She blinked. "Wow, it sure is the king of all pool toys! Good job, Chuckie!"

"Yeah," said Angelica. "You *did* do a good job, Chuckie." She looked at everyone. "You all did, but I think Chuckie was the bravest. Thank you."

Chuckie stared. Had Angelica actually just thanked him? He grinned. "Anytime, Angelica," he said.

"Anyone interested in hearing the end of the pirate story and finding out what happens to Princess Angelique?" asked Grandpa.

The kids all looked at each other. Angelica spoke up first, "Umm, I think I've had enough of pirate stories and ships for today!" she said.

"I think I'll just go inside and take a nap!"

"That sounds like a great idea!" said Susie.

Phil and Lil yawned and followed the girls inside.

Betty and Didi gave each other surprised looks. The kids were actually *asking* to take a nap?

Angelica led everyone into the house. They all went upstairs for their naps, and Betty and Didi followed them. Tommy and Chuckie were left standing in the kitchen.

"Did that really happen?" Chuckie asked Tommy. "Or was it just a dream?"

"It feels like it happened," Tommy said. "'Sides, we couldn't of had the same exact dream, could we? Blackbeard and Grommet and Mary and Anne and the treasure and all." Just then he felt something inside his diaper. He reached inside and found a handful of gold coins—foil-wrapped chocolate ones.

"Yo ho ho," said Tommy, throwing his arm around Chuckie's shoulder.

"And a bottle of milk," finished Chuckie.

"Mmm! A bottle of milk would be great with

this chocolate!" said Tommy.

He pointed to the pile of encyclopedias and cookbooks still stacked up next to the refrigerator. "Look! I can climb right up and fill both our bottles! Just give me a boost."

"Wait, Tommy . . .," began Chuckie.

"Yes, Chuckie?" said Tommy, waiting to hear Chuckie tell him how dangerous it was.

Chuckie smiled. "This time I'll do the climbing!"

THE END

About the Author

Kitty Richards is the pen name for a children's book editor and writer in New York City. She is the author of over thirty-five books for children, including the *Rugrats* titles, *Once Upon a Reptar, Ice Cream Fun Day, Star-Spangled Babies*, and *Hang on to Your Diapies, Babies, We're Going In!* Kitty lives near the Hudson River, where she keeps a constant lookout for pirate ships. She was inspired to write *Yo Ho Ho and a Bottle of Milk* after reading the swashbuckling tale of Anne Bonny and Mary Read. When Kitty was younger, she had a childhood business running kid's birthday parties and her specialty was— you guessed it—treasure hunts!

Here's a sample of the first book in
The Rugrats Files series:

CASE OF THE MISSING GOLD

"Angelica," said Lil, licking her lips, "can I have a bite of your Reptar Bar? Please?"

"Sorry," said Angelica, "there's only enough for me." She stuffed the rest of the chocolate into her mouth.

"I wish *we* had Reptar Bars," said Phil.

"Well," said Angelica, swallowing, "alls you got to do is go to the store and give them some monies, and they'll give you Reptar Bars."

"But, Angelica," said Chuckie sadly, "we don't *gots* any monies."

"Then I guess you don't get any Reptar Bars!" she answered, laughing. Reaching into her backpack, Angelica pulled out her doll, Cynthia, and began to brush her hair.

"Hey, I gots an idea," said Tommy. "Grandpa said gold nuggets are worth lots of monies, right?"

"Right . . ." said Chuckie, Phil, and Lil.

"And if you have gold, you can buy anything you want!"

"Right . . ." said Chuckie, Phil, and Lil.

"So alls we gots to do is find some gold nuggets! Then we'll have monies to buy lots of Reptar Bars!"

Angelica stopped playing and listened. If I had a lot of gold, she thought, I could buy the Cynthia Workout Center and the Cynthia Swimming Pool and the Cynthia Luxury Mansion . . .

"But how are we gonna find gold, Tommy?" asked Chuckie.

Tommy thought. "Well, Grandpa said the shorty-niners had to dig for it. So first we gotta get our digging tools. C'mon, let's go out to the sandbox."

Angelica hopped up and pulled on her backpack. "Wait up, babies," she said. "You need me to help you find gold." And I'll keep it all for myself, she thought.